Dash!

Young Black Refugee & Migration Stories

Young Black Refugee & Migration Stories

Irshad Abdal-Haqq

Dash!
Copyright © 2021 Irshad Abdal-Haqq
All Rights Reserved
Published by Unsolicited Press
Printed in the United States of America.
First Edition 2021.

No part of this book may be used or reproduced in any manner whatsoever without written permission except in the case of brief quotations embodied in critical articles or reviews.

Attention schools and businesses: for discounted copies on large orders, please contact the publisher directly. Books are brought to the trade by Ingram.

For information contact:
Unsolicited Press
Portland, Oregon
www.unsolicitedpress.com
orders@unsolicitedpress.com
619-354-8005

Cover Designer: Kathryn Gerhardt
Editor: Kristen Marckmann

ISBN: 978-1-950730-75-9

This is dedicated to refugees and migrants from across the earth, from time immemorial.

Contents

Introduction	1
Dash!	3
Brother Man	16
Shamika on the Bridge	34
Nathan's Ark	58
The Legend of Cherokee Joe	87
A Sorcerer's Mirage	115
Obliterated	140
Story Notes	160
Acknowledgments	178
About the Author	180
About the Press	181

Introduction

REFUGEES AND MIGRANTS fleeing slavery, genocide, or economic devastation are as common a news topic as the daily weather forecast. Images of desperate souls from lands near and far on perilous treks across desolate landscapes or jammed into boats, trucks, and makeshift child-detention centers often dominate newscasts everywhere. But it was not so long ago that millions of abused African Americans endured similar hardships.

The stories in this specialized and unconventional collection are about young black people on the run—running, hiding, and hustling for their very survival. They incorporate aspects of culture and history that may be new to some readers, reaffirming to others, but hopefully engaging for all. With each story, a humanitarian concern is imagined within the realm of sobering truths about America—truths that expand the narrative of history by presenting threads of reality that often have been hidden or ignored. And the legacy of minimizing the relevance of communities living on the margins of the American Dream continues to this day, as economic policies devoid of compassion force vast numbers of low-income people to migrate out of their ancestral neighborhoods because of gentrification.

The portrayals presented in these stories link the past hardships of black refugees and migrants, and the causes of those hardships, with the hardships of contemporary refugees and migrants. Because of this, they have the potential of transforming the way some of us will perceive and respond to future humanitarian crises as they unfold. If we can identify with the suffering of others, perhaps we will be able to more readily empathize with and demand justice for them.

The *Story Notes* at the end of the book include background information and suitable questions for facilitating further discussion and research. Educators of young adults may find them especially helpful in planning lessons, classroom activities, and assignments.

Lastly, while these stories emphasize past and present impacts of forced migration on young black characters, their complex and distinctive themes make them suitable reading for adults of any age or ethnicity.

Irshad Abdal-Haqq
Washington, DC
Spring 2021

Dash!

ARABELLA IS WHAT folks call me. *That's Arabella, the youngest child of the man we call "Horse" in English*, is what they say as I walk by. I usually just look down or away and act as if I don't see or hear them. My daddy is the undisputed leader of our people, "a peculiar tribe of refugees on the run," he says. They all call him Horse, and I usually call him Horse, too. His other nine children, all boys, must call him papa, or dad, or sir. But I get to call him Horse. And when I'm feeling lighthearted, I call him *Papa Horse*. That's when he smiles broadly, exposing the wide gap between his gleaming two front teeth. He then stares with his big hickory brown eyes into my own hickory brown eyes, until I'm blushing like a ripe tomato. At least that's how Mama describes us. I cover my face with both hands and giggle, and giggle, and giggle some more, all the while peeking between my fingers. If he stares too long, I yell for him to stop and he laughs loud and hard. We have teased this way since I was knee-high to a grasshopper. And because of my shyness, he gave me the nickname *Bashful*. Only when he's *Papa Horse* does he call me that. "Alrighty, Bashful," he says, "Papa Horse has got important business that needs tending to anyway." He always ends it like that. But when we're not teasing and he's just plain old Horse, sometimes he calls me *Precious One*, or *Golden Baby Girl*, because of my light brown complexion, or by my given name, *Arabella*, like all the other folks.

Mama says I'm getting too old to play the *Papa Horse* teasing game and that he babies me too much. "You've got Arabella behaving like a nine-year-old. She speaks and thinks like a full-grown woman. Smart as a whip but acts like a little girl. The child will never mature if you keep spoiling her with silly games," she said with much irritation to Horse last week. Mama is very serious about everything. Everybody says so. She says I must act like a proper lady if I ever expect to get hitched. But Horse says for me not to worry about it. He says I got lots more growing to do and twelve is way too young to even think about marriage. The last thing on my mind is marrying some stinky ol' boy. So, when I'm feeling lighthearted, I still get to call my daddy *Papa Horse* and to giggle at his bulging eyes and gleaming teeth.

* * *

There are over three hundred of us in the caravan of refugees Horse has been leading through endless miles of barren plains, and it seemed to me our troubles would be endless, too. Like Moses leading the Children of Israel to the Promised Land, Horse said he would lead us to freedom and prosperity in a foreign country. He said fleeing our homeland was our only hope for a good life. I was told that before us, thousands of other refugees attempted this difficult trek. And Mama said we are running from a fate worse than Hell itself, but she never told me what that evil fate would be. But I believed her, and I believe *in* Horse with all my heart. So I have been marching along the trail without complaint.

We have been traveling for many weeks, even months. I have lost track of how long it has been. We move at the pace of a lazy snail. We travel mainly on foot, but some are on horseback or in the few wagons, pushcarts, and wheelchairs we managed to take with us. The strong among us push or carry the little children and weaker ones. Most of us left everything behind when we fled except for what we were able to carry on our backs. All of my important things I carry in my backpack. My doll baby, *Princess*, who Mama doesn't like one bit, but I'm keeping her *forever*; two story books and a little book of words they call a dictionary; a toothbrush, undies, soap, and lotion—stuff like that. Some of my other clothes and shoes are stowed away in Horse's wagon at the head of the caravan along with the men's weapons and trade goods. He's on horseback now 'cause Mama's got a hurt foot that's not fit for walking. So she's riding in the front wagon with two of my brothers. Three of my other brothers are protecting the rear. The *rear guard* they call them. Another two are ahead of us scouting the way. I don't know exactly where the others are, but I hear tell they made it through safe so far. All I know for sure is, I'm happy walking alongside the old folks' wagon with Princess because we'll soon be at our destination.

※ ※ ※

Whenever we entered a town or village along the way to buy supplies or even to consider staying, the locals ran us out. They happily accepted our money or stock in trade but turned us out after they got it. Thirst, hunger, and hostility have been our constant and intimate companions. During the hottest part of the day along stretches of the plain, the heat of the sun made me feel like I was in a baker's oven. And often there has been confusion among us because we speak several different dialects and even different languages. The only thing that makes us a tribe is our common goal to escape the fate worse than Hell that Mama mentioned. But since almost all of us know some English, not too long after we began our trek Horse advised us to only speak English when we are conducting affairs among ourselves. This turned out to be wise because now there are fewer conflicts and more harmony. Most of the people have been good and want harmony but a few times some of them were bad. Even so, it has been often discouraging. The thing that has kept me going is Horse's promise of a bright future.

Last night after supper, everyone in the caravan was brought together for a meeting. It was then that Horse told us the worst news I have ever heard. I understood him to say there was now a demon army of dragon soldiers hunting for us and they were closing in quickly. Until we received this news, I think we only thought of ourselves as despised refugees migrating to a better place, but not as prey being hunted. Horse said we had to move faster if we wanted to survive—faster than we ever traveled before.

"We're only one day away from the river," said Horse. "If we make it across the river, the army of our new country has pledged to me personally through my envoy that it would defend us from the E.S. dragon soldiers." At least I thought he had said "E.S.," "I.S." or some other kind of "S." I was far back in the crowd and couldn't hear him well, so I had to wait for his message to be shouted back from one man in the crowd to the next until it was repeated in my area. They say this was the way of passing along sermons and information through big crowds back in the olden days, too—during the time of Moses, Jesus, and Muhammad. But even so, the transmitter closest to me had only said the letter "S" when speaking of the demon army.

As the words "dragon soldiers" reached my ears, a loud gasp rose from the folks up front. The man transmitting the message to my area said Horse had just said "mad dash" or "mad daish." Whether that was another name for the demon army or instructions for getting away from them, I didn't know at the time. But I did know the terror that consumed my every breath because of the rumors about the dragon soldiers of the demon army that spread through the camp like wildfire. I learned they were coming mainly to assault and enslave the girls and women and will slaughter any men and boys who try to protect us.

"Even after you're sold as a sex slave and have their babies," a very elderly woman in the old folks' wagon said to me, "they will take away your children at a young age and sell them further into slavery. Then they'll force you to have more of their babies. And sweetie, you're a pretty young thing—just about ripe for picking. If they catch hold of you, they're going to pass you around like a two-bit party girl from one master to the next for as long as you can breed," she warned with her bitter chuckle.

I told the old woman that they wouldn't do that to me because I was only twelve and too young for that sort of thing. That only brought more bitter laughter from her. "This land you're in now says ten years is old enough!" she declared. "They call it the age of consent. And I've heard of a place back east called 'de La War' on the edge of the great sea where the age for taking girls is but seven. Yes, dearie, seven. They defile those girls at that tender age, all the while thumping their holy book of sanctified scriptures and revered treatises of law that their preachers claim to sanction such depravity," she said.

"Then I'm gonna get some of my brothers' clothes and dress like a boy tomorrow," I told her. "That way if the dragon soldiers come, they'll leave me alone or, at worst, just shoot me dead, which would be fine by me."

"Not dragons, honey, dragoons," the old woman had explained. "They're specially trained, swift moving warriors. And dear tender flower, did I fail to mention that they strip the boys naked before they kill them? No, dressing like a boy won't save you. Believe me. I tried it, and it didn't work. Your only hope for escaping a fate worse than Hell itself is to destroy yourself," she added. And then she taught me how to do it.

Men who would take their own children and sell them into slavery are soulless monsters, indeed. And it is they who were coming for me. I did not tell Mama, and certainly not Horse, but before I would let them take me, I would surely end my own life. It was a secret I only shared with Princess. She knows all of my secrets. So, after hearing the old woman's dark promise and being tutored by her in the art of suicide, I made a potion in a jar from the small poisonous purple berries growing everywhere in this part of the country, and I took and hid away one of Mama's cooking knives to slit my wrists. I was very attentive to the old woman's guidance. First, I would drink the poison and then slit my wrists. Last, if I was still conscious, I would slash my throat or thrust the knife into it. This would work, she assured me. But I truly didn't want to die, so I promised myself to try outrunning the demon army for one more day.

※ ※ ※

This morning at first light we broke camp and headed along the trail toward the river at a steady pace. Some walked, some rode, some carried others on their backs or pushed them in carts. I walked alongside a horse-drawn wagon carrying twenty-two elderly men and women. By midday the blazing summer sun was draining the life out of me. We kept moving but I knew we had to be traveling more slowly than the demon army at our rear. All I could think of was the sequence I would follow in committing suicide. Over and over the process of my death played out in my head. After a while, I found a twisted joy in having figured out my final escape from the E.S. dragoon monsters. An old man in the wagon looked down at me and asked why I had such a twisted and dark expression on my face. "Both smile and frown, joy and bitterness," he said with much seriousness. I just laughed bitterly and without a word continued walking on swollen ankles and aching knees towards the ridge on the horizon. He probably thought I was as crazy as a bat.

Like a trail of ants, the people ahead of me streamed toward that ridge. As each small group of refugees mounted the ridge, they let out jubilant hoots and howls. It didn't take long for me to realize they were in sight of the river. My bitter smile of doom changed to one of pure joy. But as suddenly as the jubilant hoots began, dozens of those to our rear began crying out in horror. I turned around and saw the source of their fear. In the far distance of the flat plain beyond the end of our caravan, brown dust clouds were rising from the earth signaling the approach of the demon army. Everyone in view of that dark omen shook in terror. I immediately reached into my backpack and took out my bottle of poison and knife, clutching them tightly to my belly. That's when I heard shouting coming from the top of the ridge ahead of us. Horse had returned from the other side and was shouting something being relayed down the line by one man after another so all could hear. "Make a mad dash for the river!" they all said. The command was repeated many times by everyone along the way. "Dash! Make a mad dash! Dash! Dash!"

As each man along the way relayed the message, the wagons, carts, and those on foot, broke rank and rushed ahead in a breakneck manner, like a panic-stricken crowd stampeding for the exits of a burning building. Anyone who has ever run for their life must know how we felt. No amount of tiredness or pain could stem the rush of energy that propelled me as I fled the sickle of death.

As we ran for the ridge, the youngest and strongest men among us ran with their long guns and pistols in the opposite direction to join our rear guard that would battle the demon army. Horse must have long before instructed them on this strategy. Fearlessly they ran to the very end of the caravan. Even as I rushed for the ridge, I managed to pause and look back. I saw our men positioning themselves for a shootout from behind several wagons and huge boulders.

Just before I reached the very top of the ridge, I heard the barrage of gunfire exploding between the warring factions. I forced myself to stop and look back yet again. I had to know whether the enemy was getting closer to me. To my relief, I saw the demon army grinding to a sudden stop and turning in retreat. It was clear to me they didn't think we could fight back. But we had been fighting back for months. All along our trek we had to fight off hostile forces of every type—townspeople, tribal warriors, and marauding gangs of outlaws. Horse once told me he has spent his whole life fighting for freedom. He told me we should always try to live in peace, but always understand we might have to fight for freedom for as long as we exist.

I scrambled to the top of the ridge and looked down towards the river. Our people were struggling to make it to the opposite bank. The water was shallow at that crossing, only about waist deep, but just deep enough and rock-filled to require great caution. Bit by bit, the fittest among us made it across but it looked as if many others would not. Then out of nowhere dozens of men in dark blue uniform ran down the embankment into the river from the opposite side and began to help. I soon realized they were soldiers from our new country. They formed a human chain made of interlocked arms and heavy rope. The soldiers and strong from among us pulled, carried, and pushed those struggling to the opposite bank. The hardest part was getting the old folks across, but the soldiers got the job done—by piggyback, one at a time. Even some of our horses and carts made it through. By the time I finally crossed the river, the men from our rear guard appeared on the ridge above the opposite bank still clutching their firearms. They proceeded to descend to the riverbank and waded across. Sadly, not all of them had survived the battle with the demon army, but it was clear from their attitude that they had been victorious.

* * *

"Keep moving!" shouted Horse to us from his mount. "The U.S. Dragoons ain't done, believe me. We gotta keep moving." Only then did I realize my father had been saying "U.S." not A.S., E.S. or I.S. like I thought back at the camp.

"Señor Caballo, don't worry about the American Army," shouted a uniformed military officer in Spanish to my father from further along the riverbank. Papa is fluent in Spanish and I have a good command of it, too. It's his second language and my third. He taught me it from the time I could talk, so I understood every word the officer was saying. As the uniformed officer spoke, a vast array of military force marched into view behind him. It looked like more than a hundred troops, both on foot and horseback, with big guns—canons of varying size. They took position along the riverbank.

"This river, Rio Bravo, which the Gringos call Rio Grande, marks the new border with the U.S. State of Texas," said the officer, who introduced himself to Horse as Colonel Medina. "You are now in Mexico. El Presidente has promised safe passage for all American refugees from slavery. No bridge or fence will keep you out. And we have been awaiting your arrival for many days, Señor Caballo. You and your people are safe now, just like the thousands of migrants and refugees who came earlier."

No sooner had the colonel said, "safe now," that dozens of U.S. troops on horseback appeared at the top of the ridge on the other side of the river. Colonel Medina stared up at the American soldiers, with his right arm raised high, sword in hand. Everyone knew the canons would start firing on the lesser equipped Americans if he dropped his arm.

From where I was standing, I could see the faces and even the whites of the eyes of the toubab dragoons. I began shaking uncontrollably. "Horse!" I screamed. "I want my Papa!" I screamed it over and over until Horse galloped over to me and jumped from his horse. He held me tightly and told me to calm down. "Don't let the demons get me," I pleaded. "Don't let them send me to de La War! Don't let them *take* me," I pleaded again. I guess the shock of actually seeing the dragoons caused me to forget about killing myself.

"Calm down, *Baby Girl* —my *Precious One*," Horse whispered to me. "No one is going to send you to Delaware or anywhere else."

Through my tears, I could see Colonel Medina frowning in obvious disgust as he spit on the ground toward the American soldiers. He jerked his raised arm back and forth slightly once, signaling one last time that he was about to lower his arm at any second. I looked up from my Daddy's embrace to see a man who appeared to be the American commander. He raised his arm and made three circles in the air with his index finger and then pointed to the rear, signaling for his men to stand down. The U.S. troops then backed their mounts from the ridge, turned around and disappeared, abandoning the mission to kidnap and enslave me and the others.

* * *

Now that we're in Mexico, I and the other refugees feel safer. Horse says the Mexican government is going to grant us citizenship. If we ever get the U.S. citizenship owed to us, I'll have what they call dual citizenship.

According to Horse, Mexico has also pledged to give us land. The Mexican army is escorting us to a special village for black and Indian runaway slaves, *Negros Mascogos*, they call us, meaning most of us speak Muscogee Gullah creole, or as some say, Afro-Seminole creole, as our first tongue. It's the language we created and brought west to Indian Territory when we were expelled from Florida. Some of the other refugees are survivors of the *Trail of Tears*. They speak various tongues, like Cherokee, Choctaw, Chickasaw, basic Seminole, Spanish, or English. Horse speaks them all, but I prefer Gullah and always will. It's one of the few things I do without feeling the least bit shy.

* * *

The Mexicans are leading us to a village called *Nacimiento de los Negros*—a place of new beginning for black and Indian refugees from American slavery. They say there are thousands like us settled in similar villages all across northern Mexico. *Afro-Mexicanos* is what some call them. I feel so excited and proud about it all. "Papa Horse!" I shouted a few minutes ago. "I feel so proud. Thank God for Los Estados Unidos Mexicanos! Yahoo!"

Everybody around me looked at me like I was crazy, but then they all smiled. Papa Horse came over to me and smiled broadly, exposing the wide gap between his front teeth. "Bashful, darling, you're right," he replied. "Thank God for Los Estados Unidos Mexicanos!" He stared at me while continuing to flash his magnificent smile. I turned beet-red and covered my face with both hands. "Stop it, Papa Horse!" I yelled. He laughed loud and hard. "We had our freedom in America," he added, "but they wanted to take it back and sell us down the river. Another broken treaty! I thought we'd surely be free by 1850 but here we are still running and fighting. I'm just glad Mexico was within reach. Right now, though, Papa Horse has got important business that needs tending to." He then galloped off on his stallion toward the leading edge of our ragtag tribe of slow-moving refugees.

* * *

John Horse is my Papa. They call him by many names—Juan Caballo, Juan Cavallo, John Cowaya, and Gopher John. But all I have to say is thank God for *Papa Horse!*

Many of our possessions were lost during the dash across the river, but they were only *things*. We're alive and free. This is what matters. And now that I know we're headed to *Nacimiento de los Negros*, I can shed my fear, throw out the poison, and give up this knife because, *Arabella, the youngest child of the man they call "Horse" in English*, plans on being around for a good long spell.

Brother Man

"NOBODY LIKES AMOS Manus 'cause the man ain't right. *Brother Manus* is what some call him, or *Brother Man*, or *Bruh Man*, for short. Ha, ha, ha! *Bruh Maaann!* Whatever. But the bottom line is, nobody likes him. Nobody I deal with, anyway. No regular folks. Nobody normal. In fact, let me put it another way. Everybody *hates* that bastard. We *hate* Amos Manus. From day one, we hated him. He thinks he's better than everybody. He showed up here several years ago with his damn goats—Nubian goats, *Nubians* they call them for short. You ever wonder what he does with those goats when nobody's looking? I can give it a guess, the pervert. Where was I? Oh, yeah. From the very first day he arrived in these parts, our property began disappearing. In fact, three extremely valuable commodities of mine went missing just yesterday. That's why I'm testifying here tonight! And another thing, Manus is always going out of town in one of his vehicles. I gotta wonder if our property is going out of town with him. So the way I see it he's either a crook or a jinx. Bad or worse than bad, that's the situation. We should just string him up or run him out of town. One or the other. He doesn't fit in. He's got all these funny sounding religious expressions that don't make sense. *Peace be with thee,* he says. Who the heck says *thee* nowadays? Him with his beard. Those guys love beards for some reason. And his wife and daughters wear that funny head gear and long dresses like they're so pure and decent, and modest. They don't go to church with us. They go way out to the other side of the county to some kind of spiritual meeting center. I don't know where it is or what it is, but they don't call it a church, and five will get you ten, they're talking subversion up in there. I suspect they're scheming to destroy our way of life and concocting new laws based on their own culture. But I gotta say Manus does seem to be truthful. Ask him something and he'll straight out tell you the truth. That is, if he answers at all. I'll give him that much credit, but I think his ideas are weird. Yessiree, that Manus fellow has got some mighty strange ideas about religion, freedom, and the American way. I don't even try to talk to him about that stuff no more. I get too mad. Plus, he don't drink. He don't smoke cigars with us. He don't gamble. Won't even buy one darn raffle ticket to help the veterans. And . . . and, he don't seem to enjoy the ladies very much either, if you know what I mean. But he's got them goats, though. I do wonder about them goats. Humph! The man's got to go. The whole family. They don't fit in and they don't want to fit in. Makes me nervous. His kind is spreading all across the country according to the news. We gotta stop it—now. If not, in a year from now don't be surprised to catch your teenaged son or daughter sneaking around in the woods with a Nubian! So, they must go! That's how I see it and . . . *that's the way it ought to be.* And if you folks can't fix this problem, maybe it's time to vote in a new sheriff and all new county supervisors. I'm the biggest rancher and farmer in these parts and as you know, Will Bishop puts his money where his interests lie. Big money. *Real big money.* So, what I want to know right now, is what you people are going to do about this here situation?"

After Will Bishop ended his rant at the board of supervisors' closed hearing on the rash of thefts in the region, he walked from the podium toward his seat on the front row in the town hall auditorium. As he walked, thunderous applause by other attendees filled the large room. Over two dozen of them gave him a standing ovation.

The board chairman, Bobby Ray Goodlow, smiled and stood from his seat at the long table in the front of the room and addressed the gathering. "Gentlemen, we've now concluded the comment portion of the hearing. I know it's been a long evening but we're coming to the end. We beg your patience. Give us about twenty minutes to discuss your comments and we'll address your concerns as soon as we're done. This shouldn't take very long at all."

The eight supervisors, accompanied by the county attorney, then retired to a small conference room at the rear of the building. After ten minutes, Goodlow stuck his head out of the conference room door and summoned Sheriff Buddy Giles to join the meeting. Fifteen minutes later the sheriff and supervisors emerged from the meeting and took their seats before the fifty-eight remaining attendees in the audience. Chairman Goodlow stood before the gathering of business and political leaders, all men, and presented the board's agreed upon solution.

"First, I want to thank you for indulging us this evening, gentlemen. Now, let me get straight to the point. Obviously, we all know there's a thief or thieves in the region stealing our valuable property. While we have not yet caught anyone red-handed, most of us have strong suspicions that one, Amos Manus, is somehow connected because this problem did not start until he arrived, and it's a known fact his kind is prone to this type of thievery."

"Ain't that the truth!" shouted Will Bishop, jumping up from his chair. "Are you going to lock him up?"

Chairman Goodlow waved his outstretched arm up and down, motioning for Will Bishop to sit down, and then continued. "Even though he's a suspect, no one has presented evidence that Manus is actually the guilty party. At the advice of legal counsel, we do not have a basis for locking him up or running him out of town."

"Yeah, but what about the goats?" asked Will Bishop, again jumping up from his chair.

"What about the goats, Will? Do you have evidence that Manus has been doing something weird with his goats? What do *you* know about those goats?"

Will Bishop sank back into his seat with a sheepish expression on his face. "Who me? Why I don't know a thing about goats. I'm just saying maybe we can investigate Manus and his Nubian goats. We can't just let that goat bugger go free."

"Will, again, there's no evidence of Manus or anyone else doing anything weird with those goats! I'm beginning to think it's you with the Nubian obsession." The entire auditorium exploded in laughter, including the sheriff and other supervisors. "Now back to the issue at hand," said Chairman Goodlow as the laughter subsided. "Here's what we're going to do. Starting tomorrow, Sheriff Buddy Giles is going to make stops…what's it called again?" he asked the county attorney, who whispered his answer. "Right," said Goodlow. "*Custodial stops*. The sheriff is going to keep our Mr. Manus under constant surveillance and investigation. He and his deputies will stop that weirdo every time he leaves his house. We're going to check his papers, search his vehicles for *contraband* and I'm signing a travel ban order in the morning that will require him to check in with the sheriff before he leaves the county for any reason. This way, if he's the problem, we'll stop him dead in his tracks and put him deep down in Giles's jail. And believe me it is one filthy place—filled with mice and all sorts of other vermin. I can't stand thinking about it. Our Mr. Manus won't be so pure and clean after one night in that hellhole. Ain't that right Buddy?"

Sheriff Giles nodded yes and stood up. "We'll nail him sooner or later and there'll be no more stolen contraband in Loudoun County, Virginia, that's for sure," said the sheriff.

"But sir, is this plan even legal?" asked 25-year-old Jasper Wright from the third row of the audience. "What will be the basis for making these stops? Don't they have to be based on a reasonable suspicion or a violation of some kind?" He stood with his palms turned up. Freckles galore covered his face and an unruly shock of red hair atop his scalp jutted out wildly in every direction. An expression of bewilderment revealed his disbelief in the board's proposed solution. He had recently returned to the town of Lovettsville from business school in New England, where he studied finance, some business law, and real estate. Being the eldest son of the town's most prominent banker, everyone expected he would one day control the purse strings of the largest financial institution in the county.

"That's a fair question, Jasper," replied Chairman Goodlow. "The emergency order I'm signing tomorrow will require written permission to leave town and it'll empower the sheriff to carryout safety checks on all vehicles on the road for as many times as he deems necessary for the public good. So that's the basis. This means the sheriff could, if he wants, stop any of y'all, too. But I'm sure he won't be doing that. Ain't that right, Buddy?" asked Goodlow.

"That's right," answered Sheriff Giles. "My aim is to target the one that's been targeting us. Plain and simple."

"So, that's it for . . ." Chairman Goodlow was saying when he was interrupted.

"But, Mr. Chairman," shouted Jasper Wright from the audience, "based on what I learned from Mr. Brown, one of my business mentors in Massachusetts, this whole scheme smacks of religious discrimination! I don't think it's legal."

Chairman Goodlow, now flush red and frowning, asked, "Are you a lawyer, Jasper?"

"No, I'm not but . . ."

"But nothing! I'm being advised by our seasoned and most highly esteemed county attorney. He says it's legal. So like I said earlier, that's that!"

"Well, even if it is legal, it's not right," said Jasper Wright. "It can't be right. We can't go around harassing other citizens just because they practice a different religion or have different cultural practices. Maybe there are some things about our own culture that need improving."

"There ain't nothing wrong with our culture!" shouted Will Bishop. "It was good enough for my daddy and my daddy's daddy, and it's good enough for me. Them goat lovers need to get with the program, plain and simple. They're the ones that should change."

Chairman Goodlow, still flush red, simply squinted at Jasper Wright. "Will's right!" he said. He grabbed his gavel and shook it at Jasper. Then he stood from his seat and slammed the gavel down three times. "The decision has been made and this meeting is hereby adjourned!"

✳ ✳ ✳

Unlike most farm animals, goats are escape artists that constantly search for paths to freedom. It's in their very nature to rebel against captivity. If the fence surrounding their pen is not extremely high, there are some goat breeds that can take a running start and leap right over it like a gazelle, their cousin in the wild. They are clever, alert, and sociable. Amos Manus loved these things about goats. He so much loved their spirit of independence and freedom that he wanted it as an everyday natural reminder in his life of what he, himself, should be fighting for. So, he went into the goat business. But he didn't go in with the intent of slaughtering goats and selling their meat for food like so many other goat farmers. He didn't want to raise goats as pets either, like some folks do. No, he only wanted to raise them as dairy animals, and one of the best dairy breeds in all creation is the Nubian goat—or as most in the business call them, just plain *Nubians*. From their milk, the best cream, butter, and cheese in the world are produced. They have gentle dispositions, are sociable, and outgoing. Like other goats, they are sometimes called stubborn. But being highly intelligent, even clever, they know what they like and dislike and maybe stubborn is the wrong word. Maybe they simply insist on not being forced to do things they dislike.

Amos Manus, his wife, Jessica, and their eight children, four boys and four girls, lived a plain and simple lifestyle on a small farm on the outskirts of Lovettsville. He and his wife never called their children *kids*. "Kids are baby goats," they would explain to others. "Our children are human, not animals, although they do get a bit wild at times."

Throughout Loudoun County and the adjacent counties in Virginia and Maryland, the Manus goat farm was well-known and celebrated for the exquisite quality of its dairy products. To the people of his faith community, Amos Manus was known as Brother Amos, Brother Manus, or, his personal favorite, *Brother Man*. But since each moniker connoted a willingness to help one's fellow human being, he was content with being called by any of them. Whenever his herd grew too large, Brother Man would load his largest vehicle, a delivery van, and sell some of the goats to his brother who lived just across the Pennsylvania border, about forty-five miles north of the farm. "The Nubian is the best dairy goat in the world," he had told his younger brother, Aaron, when he was getting started in the business. "Treat them right and before you know it prosperity from the blessed fountain of abundance will pour down upon you endlessly." On other occasions Brother Man would sell some of his dairy products at a discount to his brother, who would, in turn, resell them at a farmer's market for a modest profit.

Three days after the raucous board of supervisors' hearing to which he was neither invited nor informed of, Brother Man arose well before dawn in preparation for a trip to deliver several Nubians and other goods to his brother in Adams County, PA. After a small breakfast consisting of eggs and biscuits, he went out to the carriage house and loaded his cargo into the largest vehicle he owned, a new delivery van he considered a bit too ornate for his committed plain lifestyle. He bought it anyway because it was the only one readily available and its large interior fulfilled an immediate need. Some of the cargo he was delivering to his brother he hid in a secret ventilated compartment beneath the floorboards of the van's interior. He covered the floor with layers of carpeting and straw and then roped four juvenile goats to the tie downs inside of the van—two young females, called doelings, and two males, or bucklings. "You're not kids anymore," he said to them. "Time to grow up and move on." Along with the Nubians, he loaded a large food basket, a box filled with books, and several sealed crates of goat cheese.

At first light, Brother Man, feeling both nervous and assured, headed from his farm down to the main road, the county highway leading to Maryland and ultimately Pennsylvania. It was a route he'd traveled many times since his move to Lovettsville. He was not more than a couple miles from his home when, as he turned the first big bend in the road, the county sheriff, standing alongside his parked vehicle, signaled for him to pull over.

"Good morning, Sheriff Giles, what can I do for you?" Brother Man asked when the sheriff approached the driver's side of the vehicle. Brother Man's hands trembled, almost uncontrollably.

Sheriff Giles frowned at him. "I'm asking the questions here, Manus. Or is it, *Bruh Man*? Let me see your paperwork," he demanded.

"What paperwork might that be?"

"Your identification and approved travel document under the emergency order. Let me see them. You are headed out of town, ain't ya?"

"Well, yes I am, but I didn't know I was banned from traveling unless I had permission. Never heard of such a thing."

"It's a new requirement, Manus. It's posted at the town hall. If you socialized more with folks you would have heard about it. That's the problem with you. You don't fit in," the sheriff said. He stepped back from Brother Man's vehicle and looked it over. "This is a mighty fine piece of equipment. Yes indeedy! You're doing well in this country, huh, boy?"

Brother Man remained silent, looking straight ahead instead.

"Did you hear me ask you a question, boy? You trying to ignore me? Trying to get smart with me?"

"No, I'm not trying to get smart, sir. And yes sir, I guess I'm doing okay," replied Brother Man.

"What kind of vehicle is this? Is it safe? Where did you get it?" asked the sheriff.

"It's a Studebaker. They're quite safe. Got it from the vehicle dealer in Harpers Ferry."

"Oh yeah, I heard about Studebaker. New to the market. Real pricey, too. You *must* be doing quite well in this country. A lot better than me. But that ain't good enough for you, huh? You want to change things, don't you?"

"Sheriff, can I go now. I've got a long trip."

"Hell no, you can't go. You can't go nowhere without travel approval. You're going to have to turn this thing around and go back home."

"I see," Brother Man replied. "Then I best be heading back then."

"No, no, no, buddy boy! You ain't going nowhere till I say you can go." Sheriff Giles stepped back from Brother Man's vehicle and studied it closely. "What you got inside, Manus? You running any *contraband*?"

"Well, sir, I've got several Nubians inside, some dairy products, and a box of books. Some might consider this running contraband, but I don't."

"Books? What kind?"

"A bunch of copies of the same book. It's called *David Walker's Appeal.*" Brother Man grabbed a copy of the book from the box sitting on the front seat and showed it to the Sheriff.

"I know about this book. And what are you doing with a whole box full of 'em? This book is banned. It's subversive. Considered contraband in Virginia. But I bet you already knew that, didn't you?" Sheriff Giles smiled. "*Somebody's going to jail today,*" he sang gleefully. "What else you got in there, boy? Never mind, I'm gonna search this vehicle myself. Step outside Manus and place your hands up against the side of the vehicle."

Brother Man stepped from his vehicle just as another vehicle came rumbling around the curve. It pulled over and stopped behind Brother Man's van. Jasper Wright got out of it with folded papers in his hand and walked over to Sheriff Giles.

"What's going on here?" Jasper Wright asked the sheriff.

"This is a law enforcement matter that doesn't concern you, Jasper," said Sheriff Giles.

"But it does concern me if you're trying to enforce the travel ban on Mr. Manus," he replied. "It concerns me because I have a court order right here in my hand blocking the emergency order issued by the board of supervisors. The court says there's a good probability it's illegal, so it issued this injunction." Jasper Wright held up the court decree and waved it back and forth in front of Sheriff Giles's face.

"Well, I don't care what those court papers say," replied Sheriff Giles. "Manus has just admitted to me he's got contraband books in his vehicle. In fact, I done seen one of 'em. So, I'm gonna search to see what else that bugger's got in his vehicle."

"If you as so much as touch that vehicle I will testify that you purposely and blatantly refused to uphold the law you're sworn to honor. Anything illegal you find in that vehicle will be considered tainted and inadmissible evidence because you will have wrongly obtained it. And you, Sheriff, will be the one in jail tonight. Your own filthy jail, and for a minimum of thirty days. That's the law! So, go ahead, let me see you search the vehicle. Go ahead. I dare you."

Sheriff Giles stared Jasper Wright in the eye. They stood facing one another with their fists on their hips. When Jasper didn't flinch, Giles backed down. "Let me see that court order," the sheriff demanded. Jasper handed it to him. After reading it, the sheriff handed it back. He frowned and spit on ground near Jasper's feet. He walked over to Brother Man and said, "Manus, you're free to go. But you can be sure I'll be waiting for you when you get back. I'm going straight to the county attorney. We're gonna fight this injunction thing! And you," he said pointing at Jasper Wright, "you, you traitor. I don't know what they did to your head up north, but you ain't worth a dime no more. I'm truly disappointed in you." He then stomped off to his own vehicle and headed toward town. Jasper Wright and Brother Man watched intently as the sheriff's vehicle rounded the bend and faded from view.

"Thank you so much for coming to my rescue, Jasper," said Brother Man.

"Well, you're most welcome, Brother Amos," replied Jasper.

"How did you know where to find me?"

"I went by your house to tell you about the emergency travel ban as well as this injunction. Sister Jessica told me you had just left for Pennsylvania. So, I rushed after you."

"Thank goodness, Jasper. There would have been a real tragedy out here if you hadn't showed up."

"I suspected as much," said Jasper. "I had to try to prevent that. As a member of the Gileadites I pledged to confront injustice wherever it may be."

"Didn't know they had members down here."

"They don't, except for me. They're all up north, but I lived up there for years—in Springfield, Massachusetts. That's where I got involved with John Brown and some of the others," Jasper explained. "But enough about me. I don't want to hold you up. I'm sure you have a long trip ahead of you, don't you?"

"Indeed, I do, *Brother* Jasper. It will take the better part of the day to reach the next station." Brother Man looked Jasper Wright in the eye and stretched forth his right hand. Jasper grabbed Brother Man's hand with his own and shook it vigorously. "Thank you again, *Friend*," Brother Man said. "And peace be with thee."

"Peace be with thee, too, *Friend.* And Godspeed," said Jasper. He then got into his vehicle and headed back toward town, whereupon Brother Man removed his hat and wiped the sweat from his brow with a plain white handkerchief from his back pants pocket. He pushed back the long blond strands of hair that had fallen across his face and looked up at the sun, now high in the sky. His bright blue eyes sparkled in the light dancing between the droplets of morning dew suspended in the air. He placed his wide brim straw hat back upon his head, got into his vehicle, and continued heading north, toward the Maryland border several miles away.

* * *

Brother Man's vehicle crossed the covered bridge spanning the Potomac River and passed through the small town of Berlin, Maryland on the other side, which the postal service called "Barry" because there was already a Berlin on the Eastern Shore. Brother Man spent the better part of the rest of the day traveling through Maryland, but by late afternoon he reached Emmitsville near the Pennsylvania border. One mile north of the Mason-Dixon Line, just inside of Pennsylvania, he stopped the vehicle.

"Whoa!" Brother Man said to the two horses pulling his Studebaker. The huge vehicle came to an abrupt stop along the side of the road without incident. Four large wheels supported the van, and its fancy carriage oil lamps suggested it could be used for night travel if necessary. The ladder affixed to the back provided access to the storage area on top. And a pullout ramp beneath the back door allowed ease in loading all sorts of cargo, even goats.

Brother Man pushed open the sliding door on the passenger side of the van and climbed in. He rolled up a portion of the carpet and knocked on the floor twice. Two knocks from beneath the floor were returned. "Homer, we're in Pennsylvania," said Brother Man loudly. "I'm going to let you all out now." He hitched the four young goats to a rail at the rear of the cabin and rolled away the rest of the carpeting on the floor. Then he lifted several of the floorboards. One by one his three African American passengers emerged from their hiding place. Stiffened and exhausted, but obviously delighted, they pushed themselves up and out of the hidden compartment beneath the floor. Homer, his wife Sarah, and their petite ten-year-old daughter Sadie stepped out of the van and into the refreshing late afternoon air.

"Whew! Finally," Sadie said. "I was so scared down in there." She smiled broadly standing on the edge of the van's doorway. Her two oversized front upper teeth gleamed in the waning sunrays like brilliant rays of her own. "Mr. Manus, sir, is we free?" she asked.

Brother Man looked at Homer and Sarah first. He nodded to them, as if welcoming them to the land of the living. Then he answered Sadie. She was a tiny thing. More petite than any ten-year old girl he'd ever seen. "Yes, Sadie, you're free."

Sadie looked away from him toward the nearest stand of trees. The cooing of a mourning dove momentarily captured her attention. When the cooing stopped, she looked back toward Brother Man. "When can I go to school like Massa Bishop's children?" she asked while adjusting the red and white plaid scarf covering her head. "And can I eat in the dining room now? At the big smooth table?" Before Brother Man could answer, she shrieked. "Oh, oh, Mama, look at that hummingbird!" She pointed toward a red wildflower in the nearby brush where a ruby-throated hummingbird hovered with its beak probing deep into the nectarous blossom. "When I grow up, I want to be hummingbird!" she shouted. Everyone laughed. "That's what I used to say when I was little," she added, giggling. "I wanted to become a bird."

"Mourning doves and hummingbirds," Sarah said, shaking her head. "That's all it takes to turn her head clean around."

"Sorry for all the questions, Mr. Manus. Sadie's full of 'em day and night," said Homer.

"Come on you little chatterbox." Sarah said as she took Sadie by the hand. The two of them headed to the freshwater stream running parallel to the road some twenty yards away. "Just gonna freshen up a bit. We'll be back directly," she said.

As his wife and daughter headed toward the stream, Homer did also but further down from them. When the family returned to the van Brother Man loaded everyone inside and continued the journey, but this time his charges were sitting upright on small pull-down seats in the van from which they could both see and speak with Brother Man. As they traveled, they partook of the cheese sandwiches, fruit, and drink he had packed for them.

"Thank goodness for the *Society of Friends*, Mr. Manus," said Sarah.

"Amen to that," said Homer. "If it wasn't for you and the other Quakers, and abolitionists, our family would have been destroyed. You carried us to freedom. We would have never seen freedom if wasn't for you. You're our savior, sir."

"Please, Homer, just call me Brother Manus or Brother Man," he replied. "We abolitionists are just instruments of the Lord. All of the credit belongs to Him."

"Just the same, you are the *instrument* we know," replied Homer. "And I heard how they beat some of you. Shun you.

Even kill some of you and destroy your property because you stand against slavery. You folks risk a lot for others. My little Sadie here just turned ten yesterday and Will Bishop had every intention of violating her. You saved her from a horrible fate."

"That's right," added Sarah. "I heard Master Bishop say as much to his buddy, Mr. Goodlow, in the parlor. He didn't know I could hear him whispering from the kitchen. He said he had made arrangements to sell me off downstate and planning to auction Homer at the market in Alexandria. He said he was keeping little Sadie for himself. That he couldn't wait till she was ten and *legal*, whether free or not. 'There's nothing I like better than a tender young Nubian kid. The two-legged kind, not the goat,' he said, laughing. 'With the parents out of the way, I can do what I want, when I want,' is what he said. He ain't right in the soul." Sarah placed her arm around Sadie and pulled her into a tight embrace. Sadie's eyes sparkled as she hugged her mama.

"I know, I know," said Brother Man. "Homer told me all about it a few days ago. The man has a diseased heart. It sickens my stomach just thinking about it. An abomination. The slave traffickers call you *runaways, contraband,* and *commodities—refugees from justice*. I call you *refugees from the devil's workshop*. It's 1856 and this ugly mess is still going on. But I can't imagine it lasting very much longer. Tens of thousands of people are standing against slavery. Soon we're going to end it. So, I want you folks to calm your hearts. We'll be at the next way station within the hour. Lord willing my brother, Aaron, will meet us there and get you safely to Philadelphia in a few days."

"What's Phil-a, Phil-a? How do you say it?" asked Sadie.

"Phil-a-del-phi-a," said Brother Man, slowly pronouncing each syllable.

"Phil-a-del-phi-a," said Sadie. "What is it?"

"It's a big city, Sadie. My favorite city. The City of Brotherly Love. Why the name alone sings out its specialness. Have you ever heard a more melodious name for a city? Phil-a-del-phi-a, Phil-a-del-phi-a." Brother Man chanted out the name several more times. "The nearest thing to heaven on God's green earth," said Brother Man, chuckling. Homer and Sarah chuckled with him, while Sadie giggled uncontrollably.

"Mr. Man," Sadie said once the laughter subsided, "do you reckon Massa Bishop and Mr. Goodlow know about that there heaven on earth—Philadelphia? Cause if they do, they might find us there."

"They won't dare go to Philadelphia, Sadie. The law is against them there. And the people won't tolerate them either. You'll be safe there."

"Well what about the *real* heaven. The heaven after we die," said Sadie, looking up and pointing toward the sky. "You reckon they're going to find us there and *get* me?"

"Oh no, my dear!" said Brother Man. "Those kinds of people don't go to heaven. You don't have to worry about that."

"Where do they go?" asked Sadie.

"You should know the answer to that question, Sadie," he said laughing. "They go to Jersey, of course!" Everyone laughed with him, including Sadie, and seemingly the grinning goats, as the wagon rounded the bend and rumbled along the final stretch of road to Aaron's place, like a magnificent liberty palace on wheels.

Shamika on the Bridge

SHAMIKA JONES PRESSED her trembling left arm against her belly to stop it from shaking as she entered the foyer of the new MaxiFresh Supermarket. She told herself to calm down. By waving her right hand around in beat with the go-go music streaming through her earbuds while bobbing her head, she hoped to exude an air of composure. Shamika didn't merely *walk* into the place. She swaggered in like she does everywhere, with the flair of a hip-hop diva.

In the old MaxiFresh, the one they demolished to make room for this new one, her graceful gait would have been considered commonplace by the security guards. Not so in this new store. Her gold hoop earrings, oversized Chuck Brown sweatshirt, and black baseball cap with the pink cannabis patch on front, attracted the immediate attention of the three security guards stationed near the entrance.

As Shamika approached the automatic sliding doors between the foyer and main shopping area, she sensed the glare of the guards but looked straight ahead, pretending they were invisible as she continued rocking to Chuck Brown's "Money, Money" go-go hit.

"Yeah, baby! That's it, Chuck! Wind me up," Shamika said aloud, grinning from ear to ear. "I got to get me some cash money, honey." Her gleaming white teeth contrasted sharply against the dark brown glossed lips and flawless dimpled cheeks framing them.

With the wave of his right fist, thumb pointing towards Shamika, the older rent-a-cop signaled for one of the others to shadow her. A husky, six-foot tall female guard snapped up her index finger to accept the assignment and followed Shamika into the store.

Shamika, five feet tall and as thin as a rail, inhaled deeply as she walked past the aromatic dessert offerings along the seductive *Power Aisle* at the front of the store—chocolate cake slices as big as her head, stacked sky high alongside towers of gourmet pies, cookies, and donuts of every sort. Just pass the donuts she looked sharply to her right, toward the bake goods service counter, not so much to view the loaves of bread and bagels on display, but to cut a furtive glance backwards to see if she was being tracked. Sure enough, a large shadowy blob was moving purposefully toward her from the rear. So, like a mesmerized kid in a candy shop, the nimble twenty-four-year-old twirled around once, looking straight up, pretending to admire the lofty ceiling with its wooden beams and trendy track lighting. As she twirled, she eyed the frowning security guard—*Lady Cop*, Shamika dubbed her. Lady Cop abruptly stopped walking when Shamika's twirl brought them face to face. She looked down at her arm, as if self-absorbed, checking the time on her oversized, multifunctional, black-plastic wristwatch. When Lady Cop looked up from the watch a few seconds later, Shamika had vanished.

"What the hell?" Lady Cop said aloud, scratching her chin. She took several steps forward and looked to her right, behind the cake stand. Then toward the bake goods counter. No Shamika. "I got a 10-16," she groaned into her two-way radio, indicating there was some sort of problem. "I lost track of the little hood-rat that just slipped in."

"Damn it!" shouted her supervisor through the two-way. "How did this happen? You were right behind her." Before

Lady Cop could respond, the supervisor continued. "I knew she was trouble. We never should have let her in. Well you'd better find her and fast!" he added. "The mayor and other VIPs are due any minute. I don't want that piece of ghetto trash shoplifting right in front of the media. Locate her and keep an eye on her. One false move, cuff her and stuff her little butt into a closet or something until the ceremony is over! You got that?"

"Roger that!" replied Lady Cop, who then quickened her pace past the gourmet chips and continued her search for Shamika in the pricey organic produce section of the store called the *O Street Market*, which was named in honor of a historic marketplace that once stood at that very location.

* * *

Mainstream shoppers go to the supermarket to buy groceries and such, but for many of those living on the margins of society the neighborhood supermarket is much more than that. In addition to being a food oasis—perhaps the only place within miles to find affordable fresh fruit, vegetables, meat and other groceries—it supports a small but vital underground economy that mainstream society is oblivious of and most politicians dismiss as nothing more than "ghetto mess." And that was the case for Shamika's old supermarket, the thirty-two-year-old MaxiFresh the new store replaced.

The previous store, called the "Ghetto MaxiFresh" by those who scorn the poor and desperate, or the "Little MaxiFresh" by long-time residents, was rundown and often filled with drama. But for Shamika and many other low-income residents of Washington, DC's Shaw neighborhood, it was both a grocery store and a vital business center. It was in the Little MaxiFresh that Shamika had worked her hustle for several years, exchanging food stamp or "SNAP" credits on her electronic benefits transfer (EBT) card at a discount for cash—a practice that violated a slew of federal and local laws and policies. The aisles of that store were nothing less to her than what the floor of the New York Stock Exchange is to its traders. It was two weeks before the permanent closing of the Little MaxiFresh that Shamika last hustled its aisles.

During that last visit, Shamika spotted her first target halfway up the chips and snacks aisle. "Hey, Brother Man! Brother Man!" she said loudly, almost yelling, "Would you *please* help me out? I'm in a bind." She then quickly walked toward the fellow, a stylishly dressed, meticulously groomed guy with a full shopping cart that included expensive cuts of meat, an array of desserts, and a couple of boxes of name brand breakfast cereals—things Shamika coveted but could never afford. It was obvious to her that he was financially better off than most people in the neighborhood.

"Huh?" he asked. "What did you say?"

"Would you please help me out? I'm in a bind." Shamika's lower lip trembled as tears welled in her eyes. It was a sales pitch she had practiced in the mirror a hundred times and deployed successfully nearly as often.

The man eyed Shamika from head to toe and said, "Wassup, girlie? Why the tears? Things can't be *that* bad."

As if on cue, she waved her public assistance debit card before him. "This is my EBT card," she said to this guy she mentally dubbed, *Pretty Boy*. "I'm all out of cash for the month but I still have grocery benefits on this card. Thing is, brother," she told him, intoning all the historical and cultural currency that "brother" has ever meant to black people in

America, "I need cash for my son's haircut and to pay off a loan for my rent that I owe to some *very serious* people. If you let me use my card to pay for your food items, you can give me back, like, five dollars less than the total in cash."

"Five dollars, huh? That ain't much. Make it ten and we got a deal," Pretty Boy replied.

"Oh, brother, ten is way too steep a discount!" she said. "Look, honey, I'm a struggling, single mom. I'm just trying to survive." A tear tricked down her cheek as she spoke. She wiped it away with her shirt sleeve and continued. "You feel what I'm saying? I *gotta* pay these people. And I'm not asking you to do nothing you're not already going to do. Just walk up to the checkout counter and let me pay with the card. That's all. I *need* your help. I *gots* to pay this loan off *today!* On top of that, my four-year-old needs a haircut. I can't let him go to school looking all scruffy. I know a classy dude like you can relate to that, can't you?" She looked up at Pretty Boy's hair with seeming admiration, the top, the side, and then slightly in the back. Crisp razor lines. Coiffed. Wavy. Pretty. Real pretty. When Pretty Boy grinned, she knew she had him. "Can't we just do the five-dollar deal?" Shamika asked. "This one time? You'd still be getting a good deal. Please, baby? *Please?*"

"Five dollars, huh?" Pretty Boy scratched his chin, looked Shamika in her tear-filled eyes and said, "Okay, little mama, we got a deal. I'm done shopping anyway. Let's go do this."

At the checkout counter, the cashier, who knew Shamika well, gave her a knowing wink and debited the EBT card for $55.44 for the qualifying groceries. Pretty Boy paid for his nonfood items separately. Near the exit Pretty Boy handed Shamika $50 in cash. In return she smiled and gave him a quick hug. "You're a *real* man," she said, "a for real down for the cause type brother." Pretty Boy puffed up his chest, and said, "Glad I could help." He then adjusted his designer frame glasses and strutted from the store with his stuff. As he walked away, Shamika turned in the opposite direction and headed for aisle seven in search of another exchange partner. Little did she know it was the last time she would work the aisles of the Little MaxiFresh.

During most months, Shamika couldn't afford to purchase much food. She scrounged neighborhood church, mosque, and nonprofit food banks for donations to offset the growing deficit between her cost of living and the insufficient government benefits she received. Near the end of each month, when the ever-increasing rent was due, she would repeatedly visit the *Little MaxiFresh* to hustle for cash in exchange for five- or ten-dollar discounts against the grocery credits on her EBT card. It was the only way she could think of for avoiding an eviction based on the slightest late payment. For each person she approached in the supermarket, Shamika tailored her pitch to best suit him or her, and she negotiated exchange rates with the skill of a seasoned business professional and consumer psychologist.

As Shamika worked one aisle of the Little MaxiFresh, in the next aisle over Mrs. Jenkins, the ever-present elderly widow in a motorized wheelchair, might be found soliciting cash handouts from everyone she encountered with directness, sincerity, downhome engagement, and a storyline as equally strong as Shamika's. And in yet another aisle *Stamp Man* might be found hawking postage stamps at a deep discount. "Stamps. Anybody needs stamps?" he whispers along the aisle. "Much cheaper than the Post Office. I got *Forever* stamps at half price!" Many customers routinely bought his stamps, not knowing or caring how he got them.

There were no self-checkout terminals in the Little MaxiFresh. "You can't put those damn things in a neighborhood like this," Shamika had once heard the manager tell his assistant who pitched the idea. "We'd be asking for trouble. Half the items would never get scanned. Hell no!"

Rarely were there taxi cabs out in front of the old supermarket. Few customers could afford them. Instead, a group of ever-present retired gents in Kangol caps provided super cheap rides to nearby streets for a couple bucks or "whatever you can give me." While at the far end of the store's outdoor parking lot, brand new children's clothing, sportswear, shoes, and pirated videos of the latest movies could be bought for bargain prices from the trunk of some guy's car or the back of his van. "It's just some stuff that fell off of a truck," one such hustler routinely explained as to the source of his goods to anyone naïve or rude enough to ask.

Upon entering the Little MaxiFresh, Shamika was always warmly greeted by the security guards, all of whom knew her by sight if not by name. Like bouncers on duty at a notorious bar, moonlighting shotgun and pistol toting off-duty police officers kept an eye out for possible armed robbers and notorious shoplifters. While they were always ready to deal with violent criminals and thieves, they were just as likely to turn a blind eye to the business transactions transpiring along the aisles of the Little MaxiFresh or out in its parking lot. This was because every seasoned cop who has patrolled the streets where those who struggle on the margins of the American Dream dwell, knows mainstream rules can't always be justly applied where there are no mainstream benefits for following those rules.

When the Little MaxiFresh closed, the ecosystem that flourished inside collapsed, and the neighborhood became a food desert. Those who depended on it, like Shamika, Stamp Man, and Mrs. Jenkins, the disabled widow, no longer had a safe haven in which to negotiate their survival.

From the closing of the Little MaxiFresh until the opening of the more upscale MaxiFresh two years later, thousands of residents were forced to trek miles by bus or subway to unfamiliar supermarkets in distant sections of the city just to find fresh food and, for hustlers like Shamika, to negotiate their financial wellbeing. Customers like them mourned the closing, but most of the well-to-do newcomers to the neighborhood rejoiced because it signaled the end of all that "ghetto mess" in *their* supermarket and the fulfillment of the mayor's campaign promise to support full-on revitalization of the area. The so-called revitalization resulted in more aggressive gentrification and the forced migration of long-time residents from their neighborhood due to skyrocketing rent and property tax increases.

※ ※ ※

Five days before the demolition of the Little MaxiFresh, the instruments of destruction arrived at the site of the shuttered store in the early hours of the day, shortly after dawn. They came in rumbling diesel truck convoys pulling trailers weighted down with bulldozers, backhoes, and crane components.

The wrecking crew was comprised of a couple dozen men and a handful of women. Outfitted in coveralls, hardhats and bright lime and silver safety vests, they emerged from the trucks and other vehicles, and prepared to carry out the dirty deed—a mission that would ultimately gush countless volumes of dust, noise, and water pollution into the surrounding area. In the days following their arrival, the crane was erected with its monstrous wrecking ball on target to strike the first lethal blow against the doomed building, but the demolition crew was on orders not to begin until after the mayor's groundbreaking ceremony at high noon of the fifth day.

Shortly before noon of that fateful day, neighborhood residents from both sides of the social and economic divide came out to witness the ceremony. Under a clear sky and blinding sun, Mayor Winston Brown exited his limousine and stood before a portable podium equipped with a microphone and large speakers on each side. He welcomed everyone to the ceremony and described the scope of the development that would take place at the site. He then specifically acknowledged by name many of the political and business dignitaries who claimed a stake in the project. Amid sporadic applause, Mayor Brown slipped on a pair of new crystal-clear safety goggles and black leather work gloves. He then walked over to a sparkling new jackhammer with a huge red bow affixed to its front. With the help of the construction company supervisor he took the jackhammer from its stand with both hands and stuck its point into a predrilled opening in the ground. He squeezed the starter lever of the jackhammer and laughed aloud as it sliced through the crumbling asphalt of the supermarket's decrepit parking lot. A dozen of the city's political bosses and business leaders applauded and watched in amusement as the vibrating machine shook the mayor around like a rodeo cowboy atop a bucking bronco. The construction boss saved the mayor from losing control of the powerful machine by gripping its top from the front with one hand.

It was only after the noise of the jackhammer had subsided that the mayor heard booing coming from the northside of the lot. Taunts of *sellout, traitor, money whore,* and profanity of all sorts spewed from the crowd of long-time residents gathered there. No one booed more loudly than Shamika Jones. She booed and cried, and then crumbled to the ground in despair while gripping her head with both hands.

Amid the booing, Mayor Brown walked to the podium and grabbed the microphone. "There's no call for this type of behavior, folks! We've got to embrace new development and close the gap that divides us," he pleaded, to which the larger crowd of mostly neighborhood newcomers on the southside of the lot screamed their approval. Shout outs of "That's right!" and "Thank you Mr. Mayor!" peppered the air. They then emitted sustained cheering for him that drowned out the booing and cursing of the smaller crowd of long-time residents. No one cheered more enthusiastically for the mayor than Rebecca Farnsworth, a twenty-seven-year-old government business analyst who had arrived in the city six months earlier with a freshly minted Ivy League MBA. To her, that old store was nothing more than a decrepit and dysfunctional hellhole. Mayor Brown grinned when he heard her and the other newcomers cheering him on. He raised both arms high in the air while flashing peace signs with both hands to his supporters on the southside. He then slipped into his chauffeured limousine and left the area. The other dignitaries soon followed his lead. With a bullhorn, the construction boss directed all of the other attendees to clear the area as his crew erected sections of chain link fencing back into their concrete anchors along the perimeter of the demolition site. Within minutes after the area was cleared and fenced-in, the inevitable carnage ensued.

    Shamika watched intently from across the street as the crane operator released the wrecking ball for the first time. It slammed against the side of the *Little MaxiFresh* with the coldness of a guillotine blade slicing through the neck of a wretched peasant. With each subsequent crash of the wrecking ball against its target, Shamika felt a sharp kick in the gut. The endless pounding of her heart and uncontrollable stream of tears were more than she could bear. After fifteen minutes, she arose from her curbside seat and staggered home in a blue funk.

* * *

Cupcakes of every flavor and size, six to a package, were stacked into a pyramid on a table just beyond the olives and antipasto bar of the new MaxiFresh. The large black tablecloth covering the cupcake table draped nearly to the floor, providing Shamika perfect cover for her petite frame. She pushed the tablecloth aside and rising slowly from a contorted crouch Houdini would have envied, she peered from behind the mountain of pastries. She spied *Lady Cop* at the far end of the *O Street Market* section of the store, lumbering past the organic apples, decidedly on her way towards the north end of the store in her search.

    With no time to waste, Shamika, shaking like a leaf, went into action. She scurried from her hideaway to the next aisle past the gourmet chips to the bottled designer water aisle, where the latest luxury icons of shamelessly high-priced refreshing beverages filled the shelves along with water filtration systems and accessories. *Didn't have this in the old store*, she thought, with eyes stretched wide. An older Caucasian woman in a finely tailored suit standing nearby shot Shamika a side-eyed glance, clutched her purse to her side, and turned back to studying the offerings on the shelf before her. *Not my kind of peeps*, thought Shamika. She scampered pass the expansive Kosher and international food aisles only to find more of the same—*snooty newcomers acting like they're so special*. But in the new "Pet" aisle, the largest and most fully stocked one in the area, she hit pay dirt. Shamika's *Tall Skinny Girl from 'Cross the Alley* was loading a huge bag of dog food into a shopping cart.

Shamika removed her ear buds and stuffed them into the pocket of her skinny jeans and hurried over to the woman. "Hey, girl, how you doin'!" Shamika said. "Long time, no see."

The tall, slim woman looked down at Shamika, raised her cap slightly and pushed her long blond hair to the back of her head. "Do I know you?" she asked from a droopy-eyed daze.

"Stop playing, girlfriend!" said Shamika, almost shrieking, while patting the woman's shoulder. "Of course, you know me. I live in the rowhouse across the alley from you."

The woman hunched her shoulders and made a courteous, but fake, smile. "Sorry, I don't recognize you."

"You own all of those big black and white dogs and the green and white Mini Cooper, right?"

"Yeah, I do, but we only have two dogs. Poodles. Just two," said *Tall Skinny Girl from 'Cross the Alley*, nodding her head.

"Well I'm the one who plays go-go all the time. You asked me about Chuck Brown a couple weeks ago. Remember? The *Godfather of Go-Go?*" Shamika pointed to the huge image on the front of her sweatshirt. A grinning Chuck Brown, flashing gold-capped front teeth, sporting dark shades and a black fedora, while gripping his signature Gibson guitar.

The woman snapped her fingers and repeatedly nodded her head. "Yeah, sure I remember you. Tamika, right?"

"No, *Sha*-mika."

"Of course. *Shamika*." A genuine smile spread across the woman's face. "You rock some cool vibes." Her green eyes, which perfectly matched the emerald color scheme of her Patagonia hoody, yoga tights, and trucker hat, sparkled beneath the overhead lights.

Shamika returned the affection with a full-on grin. She was almost *in* and she knew it. "Listen, eh, what's your name again?"

"Rebecca, well, Becca. Becca Farnsworth," said the woman, as she looked around at the nearby shelves. "Nice supermarket, huh, Shamika?"

Shamika grimaced and said, "Right. But listen, Becca, I need your help." She then went on to explain that she needed to exchange a hundred dollars in food credits from her EBT card for cash in order to pay rent and to buy a transit fare card for her fiancé, who was returning from prison in a few days, all of which happened to be all true. "Jamal got busted in Virginia for having an ounce of weed. Gave him five years. Can you believe it? They took everything from us, Becca. I can't find a decent job. So, I've been hustling like this for the past few years just to pay rent and to take care of our son, Little Jay. Jamal's got a construction job lined up, so I think we'll be okay after this month."

"Five years for an ounce? Damn, Shamika. You've got to be kidding?" Becca frowned as her face flushed bright red. "It's outrageous," she added. "When I was in high school, two of my friends and I got caught with about the same amount and the police only took it from us. 'You kids should be more careful,' they said. Then they escorted us home. Not even a slap on the wrist. They didn't even tell their parents. A complete pass." Becca shook her head, still frowning. "That's totally messed up, Shamika. It doesn't make any sense. Unbelievable."

"Happens to us all the time, Becca." Shamika raised both hands, palms up. "It's the criminal justice system. A whole lot of people would be out of work if they didn't lock up somebody. And we're the target of choice. Think about it—lawyers, prison guards, wardens, judges, probation officers, social workers, cops, food preparers—a lot of people. The economy would probably crash if they didn't feed on us. Hell, I could go on and on. Why do you guys always act like you don't know what's going on in this world? *Nice supermarket, huh, Shamika?* Baby girl you don't know the half of it." Shamika was getting angry. She realized she was about to blow her deal. She patted Becca on the shoulder again, tilted her head, and smiled warmly. "I'm sorry, Becca. I'm not trying to put you down or make you feel bad. I'm just trying to explain the situation I'm in."

Becca looked away from Shamika, toward the nearby pet toy shelf. "And I'm sorry for what has happened to you and Jamal," Becca whispered. She turned and looked Shamika in the eye. "Shamika I wish I could help but I can't get mixed up in this food stamp scam. I work for the government. I could lose my job. My whole career."

"It's not a scam," Shamika insisted, with a choking voice. The lump in her throat was the size of a golf ball. "Let me ask you, Becca, what do you do for the government?"

"What does that have to do with anything?"

"You'll see. Just tell me. It's not a secret is it?"

"No, it not a secret," Becca replied. She scratched her chin and pursed her lips. "It's a bit complicated but let me try to break it down. I'm a federal loan liquidation officer. I assess the value of outstanding state and local government economic development loans and negotiate discounted percentage rates when the borrowers desire to pay off their obligations early." She detailed a few of the challenges associated with her job and then asked Shamika whether she understood the loan liquidation process. Shamika first frowned, then asked Becca a few short questions about the meanings of the words and phrases she used to describe her job, like loan liquidation, first and second lien positions on outstanding bond obligations, and discount rates. After Becca defined and briefly explained them, it all clicked for Shamika.

"Yeah, now I get it," said Shamika. "I don't know why y'all like to use all that mysterious language. When you put it in plain English, it's easy to understand. The bottom line is the two of us ain't so different, Becca. I negotiate discounted exchange rates for liquidating my EBT assets, and not just as a job—I do it to survive. And from what you've told me, I negotiate better rates of return than your agency. Sounds to me like you guys are giving away the store." She paused a second and continued. "I'm not running a scam, Becca. Plus, I know for a fact that you burn through more weed than Jamal could ever dream of. I get a contact high from the thick smoke wafting 'cross the alley from your place almost every night. We not so different, huh?" Shamika paused and perused the contents of Becca's shopping cart. "All I want you to do is buy some groceries, cause I can't pay for dog food and cosmetics with my card. Buy some groceries—some food, for crying out loud. Do you even eat? You're so skin . . . never mind. I should talk, huh? Anyway, buy some food and let me use my card. You don't have to do crap, Becca. I'll pay for the groceries. Just wait nearby and give me the cash outside if you want."

Becca looked down. Without making eye contact she said, "Shamika, I want to help but there are cameras everywhere in here and I just can't get involved in this—*transaction*." She reached into her purse, pulled out a twenty-dollar bill and handed it to Shamika. "I hope this helps a little. If you had a store gift card or something more legitimate you wanted to exchange, I would do it. But I can't risk getting involved in this EBT thing, Shamika. I'm so sorry."

"I don't get you, Becca. Nothing is going to happen. You're acting like one of your trained poodles. Rollover! Heel! Sit! Fetch! Beg!" Shamika shook her head in disgust. "Born to be mild, huh?" she asked with obvious contempt while folding the twenty-dollar bill. As Shamika ranted, Becca squinted down at Shamika, frowning. "Have you ever taken a stand against the status quo, Becca? Ever challenged the system for its wrongs against the disadvantaged?" Shamika shook her head again, as if disappointed in Becca. "I can tell you're a good person, but you're too goody-goody. You're so obedient to your one-percenter masters that you don't have the courage to do what you know is truly right and good." She looked again at the twenty-dollar bill, then stuffed it into her back pocket.

Becca looked down at the floor, frowning, her face more flushed than ever. "Well, maybe I can help if . . .", Becca was saying when Shamika interrupted her, grabbing her arm, when she spotted Lady Cop swiftly striding down the aisle toward them.

Trembling, Shamika whispered, "This *Lady Cop* is headed this way to mess with me. I didn't do anything wrong. If she asks, tell her we're together, Becca. Please."

Becca was still red-faced and frowning when Lady Cop approached her. "Is this person bothering you, ma'am?" she asked, waving her hand toward Shamika.

Becca swallowed hard and forced a smile. "Oh, no! She's not bothering me at all," Becca said. "We're together. Friends. Just chatting," she added, smiling, while patting Shamika's shoulder.

Lady Cop glared at both women. "Well, ma'am, there are a lot of scams and shams going on," she said to Becca, while staring at Shamika. "You gotta be real careful not to get conned," she warned. "Did I just see money changing hands? What was that about?" she asked Becca.

"That is none of *your* business!" Becca snapped, with fists on both hips. "I told you we're together. And if you don't leave us alone, I'm going sue you and your company for harassment. Do you understand?"

Lady Cop immediately stepped back. "Sorry to interrupt, ma'am," she said to Becca, while squinting at Shamika. As she turned to walk away, new instructions blared from her two-way radio. *The mayor has arrived. More people than I thought. Forget the hood-rat. Report to the O Street Market section of the store on the double!* As Lady Cop started up the aisle, she turned toward the two women again and formed a "v" with her fingers. She pointed toward her own eyes with the v and then toward Shamika and Becca. "I'll be keeping an eye on you two," she warned. Then she pointed to the security camera overhead—a darkened half-dome glass fixture on the ceiling. "I will be watching. How do you think we found you?" she said to Shamika.

Becca's eyes grew as wide as saucers. When Lady Cop was out of earshot, she said, "Did you hear that Shamika? They're watching us! I'm sorry but I can't do the EBT cash exchange. I'm not doing it."

Shamika frowned and looked up at the surveillance camera. "I understand," she said. "Thanks for having my back. That guard has it in for me." She then looked Becca directly in the eye. "I'm sorry I said all those things about you being a tamed pet. I don't even know you very well. It's just so hard. I don't know what I'm going to do, Becca. I'm just about out of time."

Becca felt somewhat redeemed for having helped Shamika beyond the twenty dollars. "No worries," she said just as the store manager began announcing over the intercom that all customers were invited to witness the mayor's grand opening ceremony in the organic produce section of the store. "Let's go see what the mayor has to say?" she suggested. "I'm a big supporter." To which Shamika replied, "Ewww," but agreed to go along with her. Becca grabbed her shopping cart and the odd-looking duo, short and tall, black and white, unapologetically ethnic and comfortably privileged, headed for the *O Street Market* section of the store.

※ ※ ※

Mayor Brown, accompanied by an entourage of aides, business and community leaders, and media types, began his remarks by acknowledging the stunning beauty of the new supermarket. In typical fashion, he thanked all of the right people and entities for their role in developing the site of the store and expressed special gratitude to the multinational corporation that owns the MaxiFresh Supermarket chain.

"This new supermarket, in fact this entire *City Market* complex with its coming luxury hotel and condominium units, will enhance the quality of life in the historic Shaw community, just as I've pledged," said Mayor Brown. "As noted by one of our development partners, this complex will serve as a magnificent bridge—a bridge to Downtown, Penn Quarter, Chinatown, Logan Circle, and even LeDroit Park, which are all nearby neighborhoods in the midst of revitalization. So, we're expecting thousands of shoppers, mostly new to our city, to do their grocery shopping here at this upscale retail center. And I'd like each one of you," said the mayor, pointing toward several people in attendance, "to be an ambassador on this . . . this bridge. This bridge to unlimited prosperity!"

Then, as the mayor cut the ceremonial red ribbon with a pair of giant scissors, signaling the official opening of the supermarket, everyone applauded.

"We've come a long way from the days of old," Mayor Brown said, handing off the ceremonial scissors to an assistant.

"Is there anyone here who regularly shopped at the Ghet . . ., er, Little MaxiFresh that used to stand on his location?" he asked. No one replied. So, he asked again. "Isn't there *anyone* who regularly shopped at the former store?"

Shamika haltingly raised her hand. "I did! It was straight up chill! Awesome!" she shouted. "Most of the other regulars have migrated out of the area because of the high rent. But I'm still here. Thinking about leaving, too, but, yeah, hundreds of us loved that old store," she added.

The mayor chuckled. "Come on up here, young lady. I've got a surprise for you." Shamika swaggered from the crowd of onlookers to join the mayor up front. They shook hands as she told him her name. "Ms. Jones, as a token of the city's regard for the long-time residents of Shaw, I present you with this $100 MaxiFresh Supermarket gift card," said the mayor. He flashed a broad smile for the cameras as he handed the gift card to Shamika.

"Thank you very much, Mr. Mayor," Shamika gushed. "Just what I need!"

"Isn't this a great help to you?" asked the mayor.

"Well, Mayor Brown, this does help a *little*. The old store was closed two years ago—so it's been hard. Two years of bus fares across town added up. But this does help a *teeny* bit." She held up her left fist and extended her index finger and thumb to form a near pinch, while smiling. "A teeny, tiny, bit."

The mayor first appeared to suppress a frown, but then burst into laughter in apparent admiration for her hustling skill and called for another $100 gift card. He presented it to Shamika and announced that several more gift cards would be presented to lucky MaxiFresh customers by random drawings in coming weeks.

"Is there anything more you'd like share with us, Ms. Jones?" asked the mayor.

"Mr. Mayor. I just want to say thank you and, well, one love," said Shamika, flashing a peace sign with her right hand. "We are all one! Right now, I don't feel very welcome here, know what I mean? They got some mean cops patrolling this joint." She stretched her eyes widely and looked directly at *Lady Cop*, standing to their rear. The mayor picked up on the signification and eyeballed *Lady Cop*, too. Becca giggling loudly from the audience tried to muffle her laughter with both hands. "No, this store ain't *mine* like the *Little MaxiFresh* was. But maybe it will get better if we show love to all—like one for all. One love!"

"Shamika, I have a good feeling about you," said the mayor, now calling her by her given name. "I suspect you're going to play an important role in bringing this community together. We need more residents like you in the area. And I just want to emphasize that this store is as much yours as anyone's. If anyone ever mistreats or discriminates against you in this store, contact my office! We're not having it," he said glaring again at Lady Cop. The mayor looked to his right for one of his aides. "Saleem, give Shamika one of your business cards. If she calls you to complain, let me know and we'll look into it right away," he promised. He shook Shamika's hand again and looked toward the attendees. "Thank you everyone for coming out," he said, closing out the ceremony. The mayor waved goodbye to everyone and flashed his signature smile again toward the cameras, but Lady Cop, still standing in the rear, wasn't smiling at all.

To Shamika's keen street savvy eye, Mayor Brown's forced smile belied the sadness lurking beneath the surface—a heavy familiar sadness that haunted many in the ever-shrinking pool of long-time Shaw residents she had known for most of her life. To the world, they showed a confident smile, as if they didn't have a worry in the world. But among themselves, she knew they mourned bitterly and endlessly.

As the mayor began a guided tour of the store flanked by an entourage of designer suits, semi-automatic pistols, oversized egos, and big money, Shamika and Becca headed for the automated teller machine at the front of the store.

"Give me back my twenty dollars," said Becca, while pushing her shopping cart.

"What twenty dollars?" said Shamika.

Becca stopped walking and squinted at Shamika, almost frowning.

"Oh, that twenty dollars," Shamika said. She pulled the money from her pocket and pretended to hand to Becca, but snatched it back a couple times, giggling.

"Yeah, that twenty dollars!" said Becca. "I'm not cashing out a dime for your gift cards until I get my money back."

"But Becca, I thought this was a gift. I shouldn't have to give it back."

"I'm not cashing out a dime until I get my money back," Becca repeated, bobbing her head, right fist on her hip. "We're on a real tight budget. I owe hundreds of thousands in school loans, our monthly mortgage is enormous, and don't even get me started on veterinarian and dog grooming bills. There's no end to them. I can juggle things around in exchange for your gift cards, but I need every buck I can get, so fork over the twenty."

"Hmm, sounds like you're in a tough spot, too," said Shamika, staring into Becca's eyes while grinning. "Vet bills, huh? Well, that's what you get for buying all those giant dogs."

"There are only two, Shamika. Yin and Yang. That's not a lot and they're not very large."

"Okay, Ms. Hard-ass, let's do this!" Shamika replied, finally handing over the money and waving the gift cards in the air. "You know you could have just held back twenty dollars from our gift card cash exchange without all the drama, right?"

"It wouldn't be the same," Becca insisted.

"You're right, Becca" Shamika said softly. "You'd make a good hustler," she added. "In fact, we could be a team. You can distract the rent-a-cops while I work the customers. What do you think?"

Becca rolled her eyes, as they stood before the ATM. "Yeah, right. I'd probably have a heart attack." She looked at her new friend and offered an alternative arrangement. "How about you distract the rent-a-cops and I hustle the customers? How about that?"

"Yeah, I can see you now," Shamika said, almost shrieking, "decked out in your *posh Patagonia activewear,*" which she emphasized with a mock British accent, "begging snooty newcomers to help out a struggling business school grad with a hungry pack of poodles by trading cash for food stamps!"

They both reflected on that scenario for a couple seconds and then exploded in raucous laughter as Becca inserted her bankcard into the machine.

Nathan's Ark

NATHAN SINCLAIR FELL asleep while awaiting the return of his parents from the sharecroppers' union meeting. He had worked all day in the searing heat chopping cotton on Charlie Whitman's farm and by midnight he couldn't fight off sleep's beckoning embrace any longer. But thirty minutes later, a man banging on the front door, loud and insistent, woke him in more ways than one.

"Open up in there!" shouted the man, as he banged. "Open up right now!"

Nathan jumped up from his narrow bed and rushed to the door. He knew the crew of white men standing before him. Charlie Whitman, the landowner with whom his family sharecropped, Sheriff Chambers, and two of his deputies, Ollie Turner and Fred Smoot, formed a gang of four. They walked into the house without being invited. At first the sheriff did all the talking.

"Boy, we're here to tell you about a situation involving your folks," said the sheriff. "They got uppity with the authorities tonight and you know that kind of behavior often doesn't end well."

Nathan's eyes widened, his jaw dropped open, nearly to the floor. He grabbed his head with both hands. "What happened, sir? Where are my folks now?" he asked, almost shouting.

"You best keep a cool head, Nathan, and settle down" warned the sheriff. "You've got some serious business to tend to between now and high noon. Your folks were part of the mob that attacked us peace officers down at that troublemaking church in town. You know the one. We had to open fire on 'em when they disobeyed orders to disperse. A bunch of people got hurt, including your folks. And so . . . I had to *pronounce* 'em. Both of 'em."

"Pronounce?" asked Nathan.

"It means I had to pronounce 'em *dead*," answered Sheriff Chambers.

"Had to pronounce more than two-hundred others, too," added Charlie Whitman.

"A grand total of two hundred thirty-seven to be exact," said Deputy Smoot.

"You'll find your folks' remains on the riverbank where Jasper Creek feeds into it," said Sheriff Chambers. "If you don't fetch 'em by noon, we're just going to throw 'em in the river."

Nathan's eyes narrowed into a squint. "Throw them in the river!" he shouted. "Why are you telling me this? Why did you even come out here?"

"Watch your tone, boy," warned Charlie Whitman, waving his finger in Nathan's face. "I'll tell you *why* we're here," he said sternly. "I'll lay it out for you real clear. A heap of colored field-hands are gone, including your ma and pa. But endless tons of cotton out in my fields still need picking. Your folks owed me five hundred dollars worth of crop and rent. Now *you* owe *me* what they owed. So, I'm here to make it clear to you that you gotta work off that debt, plus any added on by you. That's *why* we came out. To lay out the facts of life. You being so young, I figured you might not understand how these things work. So now you know." Only when he finished speaking did he lower his finger from Nathan's face. Then he lifted it again. "And don't even think of trying to leave the county without my permission. If you do . . ."

"If you do, boy, I'll hunt you down like a dog!" the sheriff warned. "There's no place in Arkansas where you can hide that I won't find you. Until all of the debt is paid, Mr. Whitman owns your black hide. Try to run and you just might end up in the river, too."

"That would make you number two thirty-eight," said Deputy Turner, grinning. "Two-three-eight," he repeated while flashing the individual numbers in Nathan's face using his fingers.

"You got two days to put your folks away proper, then I expect to see you working off what's owed me. Not a penny less," Charlie Whitman said. He pulled a small rope of chewing tobacco from his shirt pocket and bit from it. "C'mon guys let's move on to the next house," he ordered.

The gang of four, still frowning, turned and left the Sinclair family's shotgun shack as Nathan stood in silence, staring at the floor, with tears streaming down his face. He closed the door and walked over to the supper table and sat down in one of the four rickety wooden chairs positioned around it. He cradled his head in his hands, elbows on the table, and recalled his parents' instructions to him before they left for the meeting that evening. They told him unionizing the sharecroppers was dangerous business, but justice demanded they try. They showed him where they kept a secret stash of cash in an old coffee can in the woodshed. They said if they got locked up, he was to bail them out. But if they got lynched or otherwise *kilt*, he was to take the money and run.

"Don't worry about no funeral or proper burial," said his father. "You won't have time for death rituals, no matter how important they might seem to you at the time. To save your own life, you'll have to run, son. Just run—like all the thousands that have been migrating from these parts over the past few years. Run in the dead of night before they even know you're gone. Hitch a ride and get yourself to the nearest train depot. Don't take a bus. It's too easy to track down and stop a bus. A train is safer. Call your sister in New York after you're well on your way. Get out of the South and don't ever come back!"

So, in the wee hours of the night, seventeen-year-old Nathan Sinclair snuck out of town while the demons of death were still busy mopping up the buckets of blood they had just spilled. Along the state highway, Nathan hitched a ride to Pine Bluff with a black trucker. From there he was able to buy an early morning one-way ticket to New York aboard the *Royal Zephyr Express* operated by the Chicago & Burlington Railroad Company. The Jim Crow car in which he was seated had a prominent sign posted at both ends that said *Colored*, just as he had expected. The railcar was overcrowded with dozens of other African Americans migrating from the South. And it was shoddy, stuffy, and half filled with freight that had nothing to do with the Jim Crow car passengers. But Nathan didn't mind. He knew there was no way for Sheriff Chambers to stop the train as it sped across the state border into Tennessee on its way toward the so-called Promised Land—the industrial cities of the North.

✯ ✯ ✯

When Nathan arrived at New York's Penn Station his older sister, Lulu, was there to escort him to her Harlem apartment.

"Thank goodness you got here safe!" Lulu said as Nathan stepped from the train. They warmly embraced. "Did you have any trouble on the train?" she asked.

"Not really," Nathan replied, "except I almost got off in New Jersey. When the conductor shouted *New-Ark Penn Station*, I thought he was saying New York Penn Station. Folks talk funny up here. I can hardly understand a word. Anyhow, the fella sitting next to me warned me about Newark. He said I'd better be careful if I'm going there. *Watch your back, young man. Newark is the meanest city in America*, he said. That's when I actually heard the difference in the pronunciation and stayed on the train. I had always heard New York was the meanest city."

"I don't know that you can say which place is the meanest. Any place can be mean, Nathan. It depends on the people who live there," Lulu said. "But even so, many New Yorkers are scared to death of Newark. Won't go there. Them Negroes is plum crazy. They got lots of factories and lots of jobs, but you stay away from it, you hear? They crazy. And they militant. Last week there was a race riot. A bunch of people got kilt, cops included. Plum crazy and militant. Nothing but trouble over there. All you know about is living out in the country, so listen to me. I'm telling you right. You listening to me?"

"Yeah, I'm listening."

"Stay away from that place."

* * *

When Lulu and Nathan boarded the A-Train to Harlem from Penn Station, Nathan automatically looked for the segregated seating area. "Where's the colored section?" he asked. Lulu chuckled and explained that there was no segregated seating in New York's subway system. During their thirty-minute ride uptown, the siblings wept as Nathan detailed the lynching of their parents and his desperate escape. They emerged from the subway at the 135th Street station. Lulu's apartment building in the 400 block of Lenox Avenue was only a two and a half block walk from the station. Less than a block from their destination, Nathan saw what he thought was a drunken man staggering around in the middle of the busy avenue. Nathan stopped, put his satchel down and stared at the man, who had just barely missed getting hit by a bus. Then a blue Chevy swerved to avoid him. "Almost a goner," said a disembodied voice from an apartment window overhead. Staggering to the side, lunging forward, leaning back, two steps back, three steps forward, the zombie walking man was circling in the midst of traffic as sidewalk spectators standing in front of nearby bodegas, barber shops, and tenement buildings simply watched.

Lulu soon realized the Nathan wasn't at her side. She turned and looked back. "What are you stopping for?" she yelled.

"Look at that drunk man in the middle of the street, Sis. He's fixing to get hurt out there. Shouldn't we help him?"

"He ain't drunk, Nathan. Just another junkie nodding out on heroin. Riding the white horse is what I call it," Lulu said. "That's what happens to dope fiends, Nathan. We can't help him. Don't you become like him. Now pick up your bag and let's go!"

"But, Louise . . ." he said, almost more disturbed by her reaction than the endangered junkie.

"But, nothing, Nathan. You can lose your own life fooling around out there. Let's go!"

Nathan picked up his satchel and raced to catch up with Lulu. They passed endless rows of small storefront businesses along the way. Nathan, as wide-eyed and fascinated as a child by the many new sights, stared at everything and everyone. Back in rural Arkansas it was culturally acceptable to look at strangers with wide-eyed curiosity as they passed and to give them a "Howdy, how you?" greeting. Lulu forgot to tell him it was unacceptable in New York. As they passed a liquor store, Nathan's country greeting and stare elicited anger from one man. "What you looking at man? I don't know you," said the man. Nathan nodded to the man, as if saying hi and continued looking. "If you keep looking at me, I'm gonna punch you in the eye!" warned the man. Lulu turned and told Nathan to stop staring. "He don't mean no harm, mister. He's new here," she said to the man. She stopped walking and turned to her much younger brother. "Nathan, you can't look at people like that. They take it as a threat. You can glance at them but don't look too hard. And don't speak to them at all unless you know them or have business with them." She shook her head. "You got a lot to learn."

"I know," said Nathan. "I'm not sure this is for me, Sis. There's too much going on and . . ."

Lulu cut him off, "Don't turn negative on me, Nathan. Each and every one of us who moved from the South to the North went through what you're going to have to go through. It'll be alright if you stick to the Sinclair principles. Do you remember them?"

"Daddy might have mentioned them to me, but I can't recall exactly what he said. Something about doing good, right?"

"Yeah. Our great great-grandfather, the African, passed it along to us. He called it our . . . whatchacallit, our *Ark*, no, our *Arkan*. The pillars that support a good life. To be kind and truthful, grateful for our blessings, fast and pray regularly, and to have compassion for those in need by giving in charity, even if it's only giving someone a kind word. As I recollect, he said if we stick to the Arkan wherever we go, we'd live within the light of grace. Just don't stare at people. And don't say nothing either—unless you got business with them."

※ ※ ※

The entrance to Lulu's apartment building was next to *Empire Superette*, a 24-hour convenience store. As they passed it, Lulu's lips were moving but Nathan couldn't hear what she was saying because the siren of the fire engine roaring by was swallowing every one of her words. He asked her to repeat herself.

"Sorry," Lulu replied. "The firehouse is just around the corner, so you'll hear that siren a lot. Like, every hour or so. I was saying if you ever need anything and I'm not around, just go into *Empire* and give my name. I have an account. They'll write down the cost of what you're buying in their account book under my name and then you'll have to sign your name. Make sure they write down the amount in ink—not pencil. And you sign in ink. And put down the date and get a receipt for me. I'll introduce you to the owner tomorrow."

Lulu's third floor apartment was clean and spacious, the furniture of sound quality though unremarkable in style. Her husband, Roy, a Navy petty officer, was on deployment in the Philippines and their only child, seven-year old LaShauna, was visiting Roy's parents in Connecticut for a couple weeks. The small spare front bedroom overlooking Lenox Avenue would be Nathan's for as long as he wished. Compared to the one room house in Arkansas, he thought Lulu's place was heavenly. That is until he tried to sleep that first night. The all-night sidewalk noise of customers going in and out the convenience store, their car horns blowing and doors slamming, their arguments and laughter, kept Nathan awake. And as soon as things seemed to be quieting down around two in the morning, the fire engine from around the corner blasted from its red brick cave and filled the night with the banshee scream of its siren, rudely denying Nathan the quiet he craved.

* * *

Just after three a.m., Nathan finally descended into the depths of sleep, but even then he found no peace because his mind's eye continued to stir. In the far-off darkness of his subconscious, he was still wide awake but in another dimension. Sensing himself trapped up to his waist in delta mud in the middle of a cotton field, he opened his mouth to scream in terror, but no sound emitted from his throat. Though unable to move or speak, he could see through the darkness with the sharp vision of a creature of the night. The earth between the rows of cotton plants lay before him as smooth and solid as polished marble. Ever so faintly chanting began to stream through the void of darkness. *Baba, Baba, Ummi, Ummi, Baba. Baba, Baba, Ummi, Ummi, Arkan.*

Ummi, Ummi, Arkan Nafs. The chanting gradually grew louder, and soon was at a deafening pitch, reverberating throughout the dark void.

From the farthest point between the rows directly in front of Nathan, a light appeared. It looked like the headlight of a motor vehicle of some sort. Nathan was certain the light was racing toward him because it was getting larger by the second and a rumbling engine sound grew louder as the light became larger and more brilliant. When the light reached the size of a spotlight, the thing transporting it stopped advancing. It turned to Nathan's right and pulled forward, revealing itself as the locomotive of a massive train in the middle of the cotton field. The train's railcars stretched back into the furthest depths of the darkness. Through the open doors and windows of the locomotive, he could see the ghostly forms of several old men, Africans, with full beards and twisted locks draping down from their heads onto their shoulders. Long mud cloth robes stretched from their shoulders to their sandaled feet, enshrouding their bodies in orange, black, and tan tribal motifs. It is they who were continuing to chant the song of the night with deep, guttural voices.

Baba, Baba, Ummi, Ummi, Baba.

Baba, Baba, Ummi, Ummi, Arkan.

Ummi, Ummi, Arkan Nafs.

Through the wide windows of the second railcar, the spirit images of Nathan's mother and father, slightly smiling, peered out at him. Crowding behind his parents throughout that car and the follow-on cars that were visible to him, stood the spirit images of countless other souls from their delta homeland. Some Nathan clearly recognized as departed neighbors who also had been victims of a lynching. All of the others he intuitively understood as being departed souls, as well. Suddenly the chanting stopped and in the silence that settled over the scene, Nathan's parents spoke to him. *Arkan, Arkan, Baba, Ummi, Arkan. Seek thee Salvation in your Ark.* Nathan tried to speak back to them, but still no sound emitted from his mouth.

The ghostly men began chanting again, as the train began to move, rumbling its way atop the polished earth, back into the void. As it receded into the darkness, its image faded to black, leaving only rumbling behind. And then there was a series of high-pitched screams, *Errrrrr! Errrrrr! Errrrrr!* The rumbling fire engine racing down the avenue rattled the windowpanes of the bedroom as its siren seared into Nathan's brain like a lightning bolt. Sweating profusely, he popped up in the bed and pressed his hands against his ears. Nathan opened his eyes to the realization that the delta train vision was over. He was back in Harlem.

* * *

Later that morning, Lulu shook Nathan awake just before leaving for her cafeteria job at a summer school program in Hell's Kitchen. She told him to enjoy the breakfast she had prepared and keys to the building and apartment, and five dollars for a movie or whatever he wished to do with it, were on the kitchen table. Nathan thanked her and walked her to the door. He bathed and ate the pancakes and sausage Lulu had left for him, but he continued to struggle with adjusting to New York. He turned on the radio but could find no "down home" blues. Instead of radio programmers with names like *the Mo' Betta' Man* or *the Bama*, he only could find Hal Jackson broadcasting from Newark, or New York's wildly popular Frankie Crocker, the *more glide in your stride* DJ. "City-boy talk," he complained aloud. Instead of Otis Redding, Betty LaVette and the Memphis Sound, he could only find Joe Bataan, the Mighty Marvelows, Joe Cuba, the Manhattans, and the many sounds out of Philadelphia, being played on the black stations. "City-boy music!" he further complained.

Nathan turned the radio off and pouted like a small child as he got dressed, but his negative disposition quickly faded as he reflected on the improving circumstances of his life overall. By the time he hit the sidewalk to take a stroll, he was in a cheerful mood. He walked along the avenue with zip in his step, smiling and wishing each person he passed a good day whether they returned his greeting or not. He didn't have any particular place to go, he just wanted to take a nice long walk like he used to do along the unpaved roads back home.

As he walked, he stopped along the way to marvel at the fancy cars, huge public housing complexes, and the city-boy shoes displayed in the store windows. While walking slowly and gawking at the massive display of electronics at one place, a man walking toward him yelled, "Watch where you're walking, dude!" He and man collided, and the man dropped the most gorgeous striped watermelon on earth. The huge fruit dropped to the sidewalk and split into numerous pieces.

"Aww, dude!" the man said to Nathan. "Look at what you've done." The man kneeled to the ground and began gathering the pieces. "I'm in big trouble now, and it's all your fault."

"I'm so sorry, mister. I didn't see you coming," replied Nathan.

"This melon is imported from Brazil. What on earth am I going to do?"

A second man walked up to Nathan on his right side and said, "You gotta pay for that watermelon, man. It's the only right thing to do."

Nathan looked at both men and again said, "I'm so, so sorry. Okay, I'll pay for another one. How much did it cost?"

The first man stood up. He frowned and said, "It was a rare specimen. An heirloom watermelon. I paid ten dollars for it. I bought it as a gift for my dying mother. She loves them."

"Ten dollars for a watermelon?" asked Nathan. "That's crazy. They cost less than a dollar back home. I don't even have ten dollars. I can't pay for it."

"Like I said, it's an heirloom. The store only has a few left," said the man.

"You should feel bad about what you've done," said the second man.

"My poor mother" said the melon owner. He hung his head and then swiped a tear from his eye. "How much do you have?" he asked.

"I only have five dollars on me," Nathan replied.

"Well, you seem like a nice guy and it was an accident. Just give me the five, and we'll call it even. I'll just have to add the other five from my own money. I can't believe this is happening. Fifteen dollars it's gonna cost me for a damn watermelon."

"I'm truly sorry about this whole mess," said Nathan, while handing the man the five-dollar bill. "I'm not working yet, but when I do, if I see you again, I'll give you another five dollars, if it's okay with you."

"You're a righteous dude, my man" said the first man. "That'll be fine, but do one last thing for me? Will you clean up this mess you made? I've got to go back to the store before they run out of heirlooms."

"My pleasure," replied Nathan. The man patted him on the back and walked away. The second man walked off in the opposite direction.

Dutifully, Nathan collected the smashed melon pieces from the sidewalk and placed them in the trash container of a small public park directly across the street from the mishap. He rinsed his hands with water from a fountain in the park, wiped them dry on his jeans, and then continued his walk feeling quite content with himself—flat broke, but content.

※ ※ ※

After walking several more blocks south, Nathan came upon a fascinating spectacle. A crowd had gathered around a poetry chanting man, Brother Ah-ha!, who was standing on a large wooden box set up on the sidewalk in front of a bookstore. Brother Ah-ha! wasn't just reciting or reading his poems from the makeshift stage, he was sing-song singing them with a cadence eerily similar to the *baba, ummi, arkan*, chant of the mystics in Nathan's overnight vision. Another man, a conga drummer called Elder Abasi, accompanied Brother Ah-ha!.

A huge Fulani straw hat and dark shades shielded Brother Ah-ha!'s face and eyes from the glaring sun directly overhead. As he chanted, he tapped on a metal cowbell with a wooden stick. The beating drum, clinking bell, and modulating chants swayed and rocked the adorning spectators into an almost hypnotic trance as the duo metered out their magic. Nathan, too, fell under their spell in short order, leaning to the left, then to the right, to the front, then back, his head bobbing in unison with the other listeners.

"This final piece is called *What Belong to Us?*" said Brother Ah-ha!, announcing the imminent close of their performance.

What Belong to Us?
I wanna know!
I wanna know!
What belong to us?
I wanna know!

Hog guts!
Don't Belong to Us!

Bare dancing butts!
Dat don't Belong to Us!

Processed hair!
Don't Belong to Us!

Euro wear!
Dat don't Belong to Us!

Toubab names!
Don't Belong to Us!

Whitewashed brains!
Dat don't Belong to Us!

The White Horse!
Don't Belong to Us!
Don't Belong to Us!
Don't Belong to Us!

Afro Hair!
Dat Belong to Us!

Dashiki Wear!
Dat Belong to Us!

Fresh Greens!
Dat Belong to Us!

The Music Scene!
Dat Belong to Us!

Nina Simone!
She Belong to Us!

Walker T-Bone!
He Belong to Us!

Jimmy Reed!
He Belong to Us!

Awesome Weed!
Dat Belong to Us!

The Yardbird
He Belong to Us!

The Freedom Word
Dat Belong to Us!

The Freedom Word
Dat Belong to Us!

The Freedom Word!
Dat Belong to Us!
Belong to Us!
Belong to Us!

"Peace and blessings!" shouted Brother Ah-ha! and Elder Abasi as they stepped down from the stage amid sustained applause and the high-pitched trill of ululating tongues.

As soon as the performance ended, Nathan *knew*. He *knew* he would become a poet and writer in his own right just like Brother Ah-ha! and the mystics in his vision. When the crowd dispersed, the bookstore behind the makeshift stage came into view. Its very name printed prominently across the doorway, *The Ark of Knowledge and Common Sense*, beckoned Nathan to enter. The front of the store was plastered with posters about its offerings and provocative quotations about religion, politics, and black history.

Nathan stepped into the store with a degree of trepidation. It looked so disorganized. Books were packed into every crevice from the floor to the ceiling. They were stacked on large tables in the center of the room, along the floor, all over the place. One false move and he feared an avalanche of books would bury him. Several customers were already browsing the eclectic collection when he joined the adventure. While flipping through a book by a former African freedom fighter on using artistic expression to bring about political change, Nathan softly chanted the words of his vision. *Baba, Baba, Ummi, Ummi, Baba! Baba, Baba, Ummi, Ummi, Arkan! Ummi, Ummi, Arkan Nafs!*

"Excuse me young man, I don't mean to intrude but I must ask you about that Afro-Asiatic poem you're chanting." The short bespectacled man with a tan complexion seemed to have come out of nowhere. "Where did you learn it?" he asked with furrowed brow. When Nathan did not readily reply, he continued. "Forgive me son, I'm being rude, aren't I? I'm the store owner. My name is Huey McLemore, but everyone calls me, *The Professor.*"

Nathan smiled at the man and said, "Howdy, sir. How you?" As the two shook hands, Nathan told the Professor his name.

"It's obvious you're not from around here, Nathan. *Howdy* doesn't come through our front door very often," said the Professor. "You're from the South or Southwest, aren't you?" Nathan nodded his head, yes. "What part?" asked the Professor."

"I'm from Phillips County, Arkansas, just outside of Elaine. I just arrived yesterday." Nathan then shared how he'd fled to New York from the Arkansas delta to live with his sister after the tragic killing of their parents. The Professor insisted that Nathan sit with him for a few minutes at his desk in the rear of the store.

"I'm so very sorry for your loss, Nathan," said the Professor with a saddened look. "I read about that mass lynching in your county. This week's issue of the *Black Word* newspaper included a full story."

"They weren't hanged, Professor. They were shot. I thought a lynching involves hanging."

"Oh no, Nathan! Any method of summary execution outside the court system for alleged wrongdoing carried out by other citizens is a lynching. Your parents, along with the other 235 people gunned down that night were lynched. Make no mistake of that. And to date, that Arkansas mass lynching was probably the largest in history. A real blot on this country's claim of being the land of the free."

Nathan looked away from the Professor, while in deep thought. The Professor remained silent, giving his new friend time to process what they had discussed. After a minute or so, Nathan thanked the older man for providing him "understanding."

"You're most welcome, dear boy. I call it knowledge and common sense," the Professor replied. "I established this store for the express purpose of imparting *knowledge* and *common sense*. When I first opened, I had a mere five books and very little money. Now there are thousands of books. I slept in the basement for years until the store became viable. I was determined to make it work despite the odds and the naysayers. They said I would never be able to sell books to black people, but I did, and I continue to do so. I wanted to create an institution that treasured and protected literature about black culture and history, and the people love it. I've built an ark!"

"I always thought an ark was a big old boat, like in the Bible," Nathan remarked.

"No, Nathan, an ark can be much more than that," the Professor replied. "The legendary Ark of the Bible is simply a metaphor for something providing refuge. An ark may serve as both a repository of artifacts and precious possessions, or it can be a set of principles and values that, when implemented, facilitates the achievement of a critical goal. You're standing in a place that has the largest collection of black books in the world!" he boasted. "I've turned this place into an *Ark of Black Knowledge*. Just like the Ark of the Covenant, Noah's Ark and the Russian Ark of treasured paintings and sculptures in Leningrad's Hermitage Museum. I've acquired a treasured collection of black literature and I keep it all in this ark. For me, the goal is to facilitate freedom for my people by imparting knowledge that makes them independent thinkers. This bookstore represents black pride dressed in knowledge and common sense. And if *you* want to achieve or protect something, Nathan, you might call the vehicle you use an ark. The train that brought you and the other migrants here from Arkansas was your own personal ark."

Nathan smiled, and the Professor responded with one of his own. "I see why they call you the professor."

"I do enjoy teaching, but I'm as much a student as anyone. The desire to learn is what drew me to you. So tell me about that Afro-Asiatic chant I heard you singing about a father, mother, and saved souls. I know a little about Semitic and African-based languages and recognized the sound of it but had never heard it before. Where did you learn it, Nathan?"

Nathan told the Professor about his river delta-train vision, the chant of the mystics, and the words of his parents' spirits. He said he had no idea what the words meant, to which the Professor explained they probably meant something close to *father, mother, the pillars of faith and place of saved souls*. Nathan thanked him but expressed deep guilt about having run without giving his parents a proper burial. He wanted to return to Arkansas but was afraid to.

"Your vision was one to be celebrated, Nathan. That delta-train was a type of ark for the souls of your people. It was a vision of salvation. So don't feel guilty. The souls of your parents have been redeemed. They are at peace, just as you envisioned them. And you fled out of necessity just as they wanted you to. They were showing that they're pleased with you. You fled from the hell of American-style apartheid. Many thousands fled before you—to preserve their *very* lives. Your situation is no different than many of our people who are part of the Great Migration."

"The Great Migration?" asked Nathan.

"Yes, the Great Migration," answered the Professor. "One of the largest and most rapid internal movements of people in human history has involved a total of about six million African American refugees from violent racism and economic exploitation. We have been migrating from the

South to the North for well over thirty years. It's called the Great Migration and you're part of it, Nathan."

"I've never heard of it."

"That's not surprising," replied the Professor. "It's not being taught in the schools because it would require exposing shameful aspects of the nation's history and culture. Even federal government leaders have labelled the *Freedom Riders* traitors for exposing the nation's shame to the world. Can you imagine that? We're the only people they say should just shut up and take it. But those days are long gone, my friend. So a huge percentage of the African American population is continuing to flee Jim Crow oppression and the indentured servitude of sharecropping in hopes of establishing a better life in the industrial cities of the North. But in recent years it has not always been working out."

"It seems to be working out for my sister. I've never seen colored folks living so well."

"Don't say *colored*, Nathan." The Professor chuckled. "Indulge me, my friend. Say anything but that and the n-word." Nathan chuckled too. "I must admit conditions in the North for many of us are much better," said the Professor. "Even great in some cases. But for others, it's a living hell. If you truly would like to know what is going on and how some of our leaders propose remedying the many challenges we continue to face, come with me tomorrow to the first National Black Power Conference in Newark, which I like to pronounce as, New-Ark. Ha, ha, ha! That's how it was originally pronounced."

Nathan's eyes widened in reaction to the invitation. He shook his head, no, and explained he'd heard bad things about the place. "I assure you there's nothing to fear," said the

Professor. "We'll be meeting at a downtown hotel. You may have heard about last week's rebellion there. The media calls it a riot, but from everything I've learned about what caused it and how the people responded, it was an insurrection, a rebellion. Nonetheless, things have settled down. It will be perfectly okay."

"My sister, Lulu, forbids me from going to Newark," Nathan explained.

"You're a grown man, Nathan. Lulu can't forbid you from doing anything. Besides, Lulu doesn't have to know. If she asks, just tell her you're going to meet me at this bookstore, which in a manner of speaking would be true. Come with me, please. I think it will help you gain a *knowledge-of-self*, and there's nothing more precious than that."

Nathan agreed to accompany the Professor to Newark the next morning. Before leaving the bookstore, Nathan apologized for not buying anything. He explained he had spent his five dollars paying for a busted heirloom watermelon. The Professor was both amused and helpful. "You got took, Nathan. Watermelons cost less than a dollar. These guys buy 'em cheaper than that, or they steal them. Then they look for guys like you to bump into. It's one of the oldest tricks on the street. When I first fled here from Manassas twenty years ago, I got bamboozled the same way."

"Where are you from, Professor? You didn't say Man-Ass, did you?"

"No Manassas. Manassas, Virginia."

Nathan laughed. "Man-Asses? What kind of name is that?"

"No, Ma-nas-sas. You're stressing the syllables incorrectly, Nathan. Ma-nas-sas," said the Professor, again, displaying a degree of irritation. Nathan laughed at him. "Okay young man, I see you're pulling my leg. You have the potential to be a scammer yourself. I've got to admit, however, there are a few dumb asses in Manassas. But let's get serious for a minute because you're not out in the country anymore. I want to tell you about some of the other scams around here."

The Professor taught Nathan about the bait and switch Murphy scam, the shell game, the white-van full of speakers scam, how to detect a scammer's partner or *shill*, ("that was the second watermelon guy," he said), how to avoid getting pickpocketed, and the "hot" watches and other items scam, that doesn't include illegal items at all. After having schooled Nathan, the Professor pulled a five-dollar bill from his wallet and stuffed it into Nathan's hand. "Today's loss is on me. Think of it as a welcoming gift to the city. Take care of yourself, and I'll see you here in the morning," he said, as Nathan left the store.

* * *

The following morning, the Professor and Nathan met at the bookstore. The establishment was left in the care of the Professor's two able assistants, while he and Nathan took the subway to Herald Square where they transferred to a PATH transit train for Newark.

"We'll be in Newark in about twenty minutes. It's located just west of Jersey City and is about the same size in area as Manhattan," explained the Professor. "But within its borders are a major airport, seaport, massive industrial area and an expansive downtown. The remaining residential areas include a significant number of neighborhoods comprised of single-family homes and duplexes that house about a quarter of the population. The other three-hundred thousand people, nearly all black and Hispanic, who are mostly recent unskilled refugees that migrated from the Deep South and Puerto Rico, are warehoused like criminals in decrepit wood-frame tenement buildings and nearly three dozen public housing projects. The projects are so ubiquitous the entire place has been nicknamed *Brick City*. If you look at the city from a distance, like from the interstate, all you see beyond the downtown skyline are red and brown brick superblocks of public housing projects laid out across the landscape cheek by jowl like captives in a slave ship. And let me tell you, Nathan, the living conditions in some of those high-rise projects are absolutely horrendous. It was just a matter of time before the population resurrected, and government officials at every level knew in advance that a rebellion was imminent. They did nothing to remedy the situation. The funny thing is that local and state political and financial leaders blamed the people for lashing out. African Americans have gone from abject poverty and Jim Crow oppression in the South, to abject poverty and hypersegregation, in Newark. So, I'm not surprised the first Black Power Conference is being hosted there."

"I had no idea," said Nathan. "Is it like that in other cities? You know, hypersegregation?"
"Absolutely. Philadelphia, Baltimore, Detroit, Chicago, and numerous other major cities suffer the same malady. They were unprepared for the massive black exodus from the south and didn't know what to do about it except build huge federally funded housing projects."

"Well, I can't stand being cooped up. I think I would go a little crazy if I had to live like that. I get nervous just thinking about elevators. And even Lulu's building is too crowded for me."

"This is my point, Nathan. You see psychiatrists are only now admitting that individuals exposed to severe, frequent and ongoing abuse, neglect, and violence will eventually suffer from toxic stress trauma or post-traumatic stress syndrome which can produce self-destructive behaviors. It has to be treated; otherwise dysfunctional behaviors and dispositions will be passed on to their children, and their children's children, and could eventually affect an entire people. Can you imagine that? I wonder how many generations of our people were poisoned by that untreated stress."

Just then the train operator announced that they were at Jersey City's Journal Square Station. Nathan and the Professor exited the train and transferred to the Newark train on the opposite side of the platform which had just arrived from Lower Manhattan. "Just a couple more stops, Nathan," said the Professor. "The conference is only a few blocks from Newark's Penn Station."

* * *

Over a thousand representatives from 286 black organizations convened in Newark for the Black Power Conference. The Professor attended as a scholarly observer rather than as a leader of an organization. The event was the largest gathering of black leaders in American history. The meeting's focus was on unity, self-determination, and on increasing African American influence and participation in America's political, economic, and cultural affairs. Nathan saw, heard, or met just about everyone who was anyone in black politics, education, community organizing, and economics. After having attended several workshops and listening to numerous speeches, he felt as if his head had burst open and been retrofitted with a new brain. By late afternoon, it was time to head back to Harlem.

"Thanks for inviting me to *New-Ark*, Professor. After this conference, I feel like a new person," said Nathan as the two of them strolled to the train station. "I think I must have learned about every single issue and concern affecting the African American community from every perspective. It was amazing. On one hand I feel enlightened, but on the other I feel discouraged. It's as if the entire society is severely damaged, if not broken. I believe I can contribute to fixing it, but I don't know where to start or exactly what to do."

"What do you want to do with your life, Nathan? What career or vocation do you want to pursue? Let's start there. Do what you are meant to do. Only you can identify that because no one can see inside your head and heart. Whatever it is, you'll think about it all the time and find a peculiar satisfaction while engaging in it. That's how I knew being a bibliophile was my thing."

"I'm quite sure I want to write, Professor. Write poetry and other things. The moment I heard Brother Ah-ha! in front of the bookstore, I knew that I wanted to write culturally related stuff, but I'm not sure that it's all I want to do."

"An artist, huh!" exclaimed the Professor. "I love artists and activists. That's why I've made my store a venue for artistic and political expression. An artist can make many important contributions, Nathan. Artists are at the cutting edge of social change. They imagine things as they should be and, more importantly, are able to present us with inspiring imagery. Just be sure to remain true to your core values. Never separate your art from your values."

"My Arkan," replied Nathan.

"You've got it, son! Your Arkan," said the Professor, who abruptly stopped walking and pointed to a newly posted event announcement. "Do you know this musician, Nathan?"

"Sun Ra Orchestra? No, I've never heard of him or his orchestra."

"*Arkestra*, not orchestra," said the Professor, placing his finger on that word on the poster. "Well you should learn about him. Sun Ra envisioned and has established an ark of black cultural identity for music and thinking that's meant to elevate listeners spiritually. His ark is a place of creativity, originality, new beginning, and salvation from the philosophy of this world, which is so often detrimental to the spiritual well-being of the human soul. Within his Arkestra there is both freedom of expression and self-determination. Sun Ra is not restricted by mainstream standards of art, music, or language. It's because of this that people say he's *out to lunch*. Ha, ha, ha! Which may be true, but he presents a new mythology that challenges us to break away from status quo conventions. We need a new ethos and new models, demonstrated through stories and myths that serve our sensibilities and promote our aspirations. As a writer you may be able to provide some of that, Nathan. I encourage you to try."

Nathan shook his head in acceptance of his mentor's advice. "Yes, I see what you mean, Professor. I can use creative writing as a type of ark, a new ark that would provide refuge for a fresh new vision, like Brother Ah-ha! Yes, I can see that. And as a refugee and migrant, I may be able to address refugee-migrant concerns through my work." Nathan looked at the Professor and shook his head in the affirmative. "Thanks again, Professor. And I'm going to try to make it to that Sun Ra performance at . . . *Slugs' in the Far East.* Gotta remember that."

"It's a jazz saloon on the Lower East Side—the *far east.* But you must be at least eighteen to get in," the Professor advised.

"Yeah, but the show is not for another two weeks. By then I'll be old enough."

The Professor smiled and patted Nathan on the back as they entered Newark's ornate Penn Station with its polished marble floors, historic friezes, and art deco embellishments.

The Legend of Cherokee Joe

"Some of them were bad." —Arabella

IMAGES OF CHEROKEE Joe and his gang of desperadoes were plastered on wanted posters throughout the Southwest. "Wanted Dead or Alive," they announced. Some offered higher cash rewards for bringing in the culprits dead rather than alive. The multiethnic crew of teenaged bank robbers had been on a crime spree in towns big and small for over a year. In the wake of the havoc they wreaked, was a bloody trail of dead lawmen, senseless shootings, sexual assaults, burned out towns, stolen horses, and empty bank vaults. Lots of empty bank vaults. On a late summer evening in 1894, after narrowly fending off a posse of bounty hunters, the band of outlaws was obliged to rest their horses for a spell in San Angelo, Texas.

* * *

The sun was just shy of retiring for the day when Kentucky Ben, fresh off the train from Louisville, fired up his piano at the front of the ballroom. He began banging out the latest ragtime tunes like it was the end of time and that by the sheer force of his playing he could propel the entire town into the deepest chasms of Hell with a wide grin on everyone's face and a double shot of whiskey in their hand. His shiny bald head gleamed like a beacon beneath the crystal chandelier as a half-empty beer mug rocked atop his piano in rhythm with the beat. And as he sang, grunted, and bounced around on the piano stool, six showgirls adorned in silk skirts, pink petticoats, feathers and lace, pranced across the stage beside him, posturing in ways that would shame the most brazen cancan dancers of the Moulin Rouge.

Painted ladies decked out in alluring fashions, perfumed and coy, fluttered about the large room trying to entice male customers into "spending time" with them upstairs. Brisk food and drink sales promised the night's take would be magnificent. And Abner, the ruddy-faced head bartender, saluted each arriving guest with a warm smile and welcoming nod. By nine-thirty the last vestiges of daylight had been swallowed by the darkness, and *Miss Kitty's*, the most infamous cathouse saloon in West Texas, was bursting at the seams and rocking hard in unabashed hedonism.

In an instant, the music, dancing, and gambling stopped when Cherokee Joe and seven of the other bandits swaggered through the swinging doors of the saloon. They brought their pistols and long guns in with them despite the prominent sign posted outside that read in standard print, *No Guns Allowed (Check All Firearms at the Corral)*. Another sign in badly scrawled longhand was posted next to the enormous mirror behind the saloon's majestic mahogany bar. It read, *No Service for Blacks, Browns, Reds, Yellows, Mulattoes, or Dogs!* The meanest of folk might apply each of the prohibited types to one or another of the dudes in Cherokee Joe's squad, except for dogs, of course, because they didn't travel with dogs.

The outlaws, clustered near the entrance, exhibited a collective air of hair-trigger edginess. As they awaited a cue from Cherokee Joe, he scanned the room deliberately, examining each face and every little thing for any sign of a problem. He zeroed in on the handwritten sign behind the bar and spoke in Muscogee Gullah Creole to the man next to him, Big Jeff, his first cousin and only other member of the gang who knew the peculiar dialect. The two of them code switched from English to Gullah whenever they wanted to feel closer, or simply to keep outsiders from understanding them.

"E look lukkah safe 'cep dem hab one buckruhbittle," (*It looks like it's safe, but they only have white folks' food*), said Cherokee Joe.

"No boddun me," (*That doesn't bother me*) Big Jeff replied.

"De ba' man, e'aa'm wid uh two-time one gun 'cep 'e so 'fraid e foot tie tuh de groun," (*The bartender has a double-barreled shotgun but he's so afraid he can't move*) said Cherokee Joe.

Big Jeff focused on Abner's face and then the shotgun leaning in the corner behind the bar. "Uh yent 'fraid de em. 'E 'fraid we. 'E werry chicken," (*I'm not worried about him. He's afraid of us. He's very chicken*) he said to Cherokee Joe.

"Dat de fack trute." (*That's the truth.*) "Ketch e' gun. We nyam an' res 'yuh," (*Take his gun. We'll eat and rest here*) Cherokee Joe commanded.

Big Jeff, with pistol in hand, walked behind the bar and grabbed the shotgun. Abner remained frozen in place and watched in silence. When Cherokee Joe felt sure there were no other immediate threats in the room, he turned his attention again to the badly scrawled sign behind the bar.

"Barkeep, what's that sign say?" Cherokee Joe asked Abner with a drawl as long as the Pecos River. "You see, these boys can't read a lick." He pointed his thumb towards his gang members. "Me, myself, I can read readin', but I can't read writin.' So I need you to tell me what that says."

At that point, the tension is the room was so high it nearly cracked the massive mirror running the length of the wall behind the bar. Abner swallowed hard and faked a broad smile. "Oh, that's a very old sign from last year. Been meaning to take it down." He raised his trembling right hand and yanked down the fading piece of paper and ripped it in half. "It just says no dogs allowed. They make a mess of the place. I'm sure *everybody* around these parts knows that rule by now."

Cherokee Joe grinned and clapped his hands together once. "Is that all? San Angelo! You gotta love this mudhole," he said turning towards the other members of his gang. Then he turned back to Abner and said, "Y'all don't like dogs, huh?" He then peered across the sea of tables from one side of the huge room to the other. "Well we just left a pack of broke down dirty dogs back yonder up the trail. And I guarantee nary one of 'em will be coming in *here* tonight."

As Cherokee Joe spoke, Big Jeff, walked to the front of the room, stopping near Kentucky Ben's piano. As soon as Cherokee Joe stopped speaking, Big Jeff, a former highly-sought-after bronco buster, held up a copy of a U.S. Marshal's wanted-dead-or-alive notice with Cherokee Joe's picture on it. It offered up to $2,500, a handsome sum, for the capture or killing of *Cherokee Joe* or any member of his gang, especially *Black Boy Jeff.* For years before he went rogue, white ranchers had called Big Jeff that and a similar more hateful epithet in accord with the local custom of applying them to black ranch hands to distinguish them from white ones with the same given name. They called it a form of affection rather than recognizing the debasing insult for what it was.

"Any of y'all seen Cherokee Joe and his boys round these parts tonight?" Big Jeff asked the quieted patrons. Folks throughout the saloon shook their heads, or softly said, no. "I didn't think so," he said. "Me neither." He balled up the handbill and tossed it into a spittoon beneath the stage. "If we find out later that somebody here reported having seen Cherokee Joe and his boys, we'll come back to visit y'all *real* soon." Big Jeff's thinly veiled threat implied the gang would burn the small town down in revenge for turning in any member of the gang. It was a common form of retribution employed by outlaws, marauders, and enemy armies. "And just so you know," he added, "a few of our boys are guarding the corral. We ain't releasing no guns to *nobody* tonight. Y'all can come back after sunrise to claim your weapons. We'll be long gone by then."

After Big Jeff returned to his side, Cherokee Joe, wanting to ease the tension, flashed his famously charming smile and turned first to the bar and then to the patrons. His deep chocolate complexion, high cheekbones, gleaming white teeth, and long black Indian hair draping over his shoulders from beneath his black Stetson hat made him look all the more exotic.

"Folks, we ain't here to cause no trouble or hurt nobody. We just want to relax for a spell like y'all. Don't start no trouble, won't be no trouble," Cherokee Joe explained, waving an outstretched hand back and forth. He walked over to the bar and slapped down a gold piece. "Barkeep!" he said loudly to Abner, "Whiskey for the boys, but just a sarsaparilla for me, 'cause firewater drives me plumb loco."

"You got it!" Abner replied. He hurried shot glasses and a whiskey bottle to the bar and handed Joe an opened bottle of sarsaparilla.

Cherokee Joe then slapped down several more gold pieces onto the bar. "And for the rest of the night, drinks are on me for everybody here." The patrons sheepishly nodded their appreciation or raised their glasses as in a toast. "So, let's have some fun!" Cherokee Joe added. "Y'all drink up. Piano man, crank out some more ragtime! And you dancing gals, let's see some stepping and shaking!"

As Kentucky Ben revved up his piano, Cherokee Joe and his crew gathered at one of the largest tables in the room, where they ate, drank, and exchanged tall tales and bawdy jokes. Before long they blended in so well, the other patrons seemed to have forgotten they were there. By three in the morning all but two gang members had gone upstairs to patronize the fancy working girls. Cherokee Joe and Big Jeff stayed behind. They spoke to one another again in Gullah Creole.

"I've had enough of this robbing and shooting, Jeff," Cherokee Joe said. "We could have been killed by that posse. I ain't ready to die just yet. Those boys upstairs, Rufus, Crawford, and the others—seems like they just don't care whether they live or die. I used to be like them, but I'm not anymore."

"But Joe, nobody *was* killed," Big Jeff replied. "You weren't even scratched."

"The reason I wasn't shot is because that third boy's pistol misfired. If it hadn't jammed . . . well, who knows?" Cherokee Joe looked up and away contemplating his near demise.

"The reason none of us got shot is because of you, Joe. You know how to handle a pistol like nobody's business. I couldn't believe how you took three of them down! Hot damn! Joe, you're a gunfighting legend! Bang, bang, bang!" Big Jeff jumped around in his seat in three directions, grinning, pretending to fire a pistol. "You were like Grandpa Johnny Horse in one of those stories your mama used to tell us. 'Bout him fighting off toubab soldiers and slave trackers. Or like his daddy, Great Grandpa Suleiman, escaping to Florida from slavery in the Low Country of South Carolina. Those men were legends. You got that in you, Joe! You don't have to worry 'bout getting shot by no gawl darn posse."

"I do recollect those stories, Jeff. But I ain't no John Horse," Cherokee Joe said. "I wish I could be like him, though. I wish I could be a hero instead of an outlaw. I don't think Mama would approve of the way I am now."

"Joe, now you're being sentimental. They treat us like dogs here. They pay the toubab cowhands and bronco busters twice what they pay us, and they know I'm the best! They call us names. Lynch us and rape our women while we stand by helpless. We don't belong in that world. They've closed us out. I'd rather sit on the porch doing nothing all day, guzzling rot gut, than live under a system of humiliation and evil. Either that or live like we been doing . . . in a family of outlaws beholden to nobody. And I know you feel the same way."

"You're right, Jeff, I do feel that way," Cherokee Joe replied. "Still, we could have moved to Piedras Negras or Nacimiento de los Negros or one of the other black towns in Mexico and done good for ourselves."

"Maybe, Joe. Maybe. I hear tell things ain't so great for us in Mexico either. That they're trying to take back the land they gave our folks. And other bad stuff, too. So, I ain't so sure about Mexico," said Big Jeff. Nothing he was saying seemed to be changing Cherokee Joe's mindset. Big Jeff returned to the subject of their common history. He asked Cherokee Joe to retell the story of their grandfather that Joe's mother, Arabella, used to enchant them with on so many occasions.

Cherokee Joe seemed to perk up. He flashed his famous smile at Big Jeff. "You know how to get to me, don't you boy? Okay, I'll tell you the whole story from beginning to end," he said and then related the family's history. Big Jeff's paternal grandfather, John Horse, was one of the most important unsung heroes in Black and Indian history. According to Cherokee Joe's mother, Arabella Blackstone, her father, John Horse, was the son of a runaway Gullah slave from South Carolina named Suleiman Baba, who had escaped to Spanish Florida in the early 1800s. There he joined a biracial maroon village comprised of Gullah runaway slaves, their children, and a great number of Seminole Indians.

Over time such villages formed into a tribal branch of its own, the "Black Seminoles." Their language evolved into the Gullah-based *Afro-Seminole Creole*, which blended English with several African languages, Native American Muscogee, and a bit of Spanish. "Mama told me and that schoolteacher of ours back in Muskogee that creole is the tongue we speak at home," Cherokee Joe explained to Big Jeff. "She said we be Gullah. I never met nobody who knew and could speak proper English better than Mama, but if somebody insulted the common language of our people, she would only speak like our people. So, she told the teacher that we *be* Gullah, the children of those Africans who *chose* to survive the Middle Passage, the slave master's whip on the rice plantations of the

Low Country, and the swamps of Florida. And then she said to me that I *be* part Cherokee, too, on my daddy's side and that I *be* both Mexican and American cause I was born down there," he added. "Yeah, she was rubbing it in. She looked that black schoolteacher in the eye—that *siddity gal from Back East*, is what she called her—who was trying to get us to only speak proper, standard English instead of what the teacher called that *bastardized Gullah slave tongue,* and Mama told her that we will speak *our* tongue–proudly and defiantly. That nobody, can tell us how to talk. That we have the same human brain the teacher has—just as sharp, and even smarter. Mama said we know what we mean when we talk. We *create* our own words. We *create* our own names, unique and *original* names, for *our* babies if it suits us. That we ain't obliged to copy toubab culture to be fully human. Nobody *owns* us, is what she said. Then she stooped down in front of me, looked me in the eye, and poked me in the forehead with her index finger and said, 'And don't you *ever* forget what I'm telling you, boy. Slab'ry bin yuh 'fo gun-shoot 'cep not no mo'! (*There was slavery before the Civil War but not anymore!*)' I never forgot it, Jeff." Cherokee Joe winked at Big Jeff and added, "I can see you never did either, did you?"

"No, I reckon I didn't forget, Joe. Thanks to Aunt Arabella," said Big Jeff. "When she died, we were on our own. Now we're here. Fugitives from justice! I never thought it would come to this, but we didn't have a lot of choices, did we?"

"Maybe not, but it's not too late to do better," said Cherokee Joe. "We could leave this off and change our ways, Jeff. Take on new names and everything. Or maybe we can join the migration to one of the black villages in Mexico the way the old folks did. Make a fresh start down there, if they let us."

Big Jeff ignored that suggestion. Instead he coaxed Joe back to the family history. "Speaking of the old folks, whatever became of old Grandpa Horse, anyway?"

"It's the damnedest thing, Jeff. Mama said he went off to Mexico City one day to plea for the land rights of the Afro-Mexicano people—his people—because some of the racist Mexican ranchers were scheming to take their land. All we know is that somewhere along the way he mysteriously disappeared—like a haint! Never to be seen or heard from again."

"Great thundering horseshoes!" Big Jeff exclaimed. "I had never heard this part of the story. Just disappeared, huh?" He slapped his palms across each other. "Poof! Just like that?"

"Just like that," Cherokee Joe said. "But I got a mind to try to find him one day. If he's still alive, he must be very old—in his eighties, I suppose. And he's got a lot of aliases, too. Wouldn't be easy to track him down." Cherokee Joe shook his head. "Anyway, Grandpa Horse, he's what I call a legend, Jeff. Me shooting down three bounty hunting buzzards, that ain't being a legend. That's nothing. And I want more. I'm tired of this life. I want to settle down somewhere. Make something of myself. Become a solid citizen, like my mama was."

"Joe, you're only nineteen. You've got your whole life ahead of you. There'll be plenty of time to settle down. A citizen, huh? With a little wifey giving you orders? 'Honey, do this. Honey, do that.' And a bunch of snotty nose brats running round tearing up the place? Maybe a couple of hound dogs yapping all night? Chickens clucking in the front yard at the crack of dawn? Well, you can have that mess, partner. But before you go off and do something stupid, make sure your money is straight *and* that you finish what you planned. That train comes through in a few days and you can't let the boys down by walking away. *You* gotta be there, Joe," insisted Big Jeff, still speaking Gullah.

Cherokee Joe shook his head knowingly. "I hear what you're saying, Jeff. My money's straight for sure. I already took care of it. Just the same, I ain't fixing to let you boys down. The train job is set to go. I got it all worked out right here," he said, pointing toward his temple.

Big Jeff, satisfied with Cherokee Joe's responses, nodded his head in approval. "Good. Now I'm gonna get a bit of shuteye," he said as he folded his massive arms. He buried his chin into his chest and drifted off to sleep in a forward nod.

But the sweet blessing of sleep's repose was not visited upon Cherokee Joe. He felt he had no choice but to remain vigilant, keeping a keen and nervous eye on the front door of the saloon. Before him the gang's assortment of guns, liquor bottles, and other gear cluttered the table like the scattered toys of spoiled children. He picked up the deck of cards that was routinely left on each table. He shuffled the cards and began playing solitaire.

By five o'clock, the saloon and brothel had emptied out except for Cherokee Joe's crew. They had paid handsomely in gold to stay past closing and through the night, so Abner knew not to bother them. He shuttered and latched the front door and then retired to his bunk in the storeroom. But Cherokee Joe, as alert as ever, kept watching that front door, while playing cards. At ten minutes pass the hour, the footsteps of Ruby Rose on the stairs leading from the brothel quarters caught his attention. He sat up and watched as she slowly approached his table.

"Howdy, Ruby," he said softly. "I had no idea you were here."

"Hey, Joe. Yeah, I've been here all evening. I help manage the girls from time to time. It's not easy," she said shaking her head back and forth, "but the money's right nice."

"It's been a long time."

"I reckon it has," Ruby replied. "What's it been, two years? Heard some bad rumors about you swinging from a rope. Wasn't sure I'd ever see you again."

"Well, as you can see, I'm just fine. I'm here because I got business round these parts."

"Business, huh? I hope it doesn't have anything to do with that harlot, Jessie Mae."

"What's that supposed to mean, Ruby?" Cherokee Joe jerked his head back. "She's alright ain't she? I told her I'd be back."

"As far as I know she's just fine, but I don't think she's expecting *you*, if you know what I mean."

"No, I don't know what you mean, Ruby. Just come straight out and tell me plain."

"Yeah, okay. I'll tell you plain. But first you gotta tell me something." The pitch of her voice got quite high. Ruby balled her right hand into a fist, placed it on her hip, and leaned in towards Cherokee Joe's face. "Why'd you run off with Jessie Mae without saying a word to me? That wasn't right." Ruby angrily pursed her distinctive Nubian lips. "I thought we had something special, Joe. I cared about you when nobody did. I cared when you had nothing. You made me feel like a gosh darn fool. The whole town has been laughing at me ever since."

Cherokee Joe looked down, while fumbling the cards in his hands. "I'm sorry it went down like that Ruby. I should've told you beforehand, but when it came time to leave, I couldn't find you." He shook his head back and forth, then looked her in the eye. "No disrespect but Jessie Mae just got to me, you know? She's got property and a head for business. She said all the right things I needed to hear. So . . . I'm with her now."

"Well, she sure ain't with you!" Ruby said angrily. She shook her index finger back and forth in Cherokee Joe's face. "You want the plain truth, huh? Well I'm going to lay it on you. The plain truth is Jessie Mae . . ." Ruby's voice cracked as she choked on her words. "The truth is she's with another man," she said bitterly. "I hear tell she's taken up with some deputy sheriff from Concho County. How you like that, Joe? Your harlot is laid up with a lawman. Who's the fool now?"

Cherokee Joe tilted his head back and locked his eyes onto Ruby's face, searching for a hint in her eyes or expression that she was joking or lying. But he saw only sincerity.

"Can't be so," Cherokee Joe said. He sat up straight in his chair. "But if it is . . . well . . ." His voice trailed off. He reached across the table and grabbed a bottle of whiskey. He lifted the bottle to his mouth and without flinching guzzled the fiery liquor—his first drink in many months. "If it's true, there's gonna be trouble," he said, after clearing his throat. He sprung up from his chair, grabbed his six-shooter from the table, gripping it tightly. Then he shook Big Jeff's shoulder.

"Wake up, Jeff," he said in English. "I gotta make a run."

"What are you doing, Joe?" asked Ruby. "You're not going to Jessie Mae's place, are you? It's not even sunrise yet."

Cherokee Joe ignored Ruby. "Jeff, get the boys together and meet me at the widow's place this evening. If I'm not there by sundown tomorrow, y'all move on. I'll try to catch up later."

Big Jeff, still in the fog of slumber, could only mumble. "What the hell are you doing, Joe? Where you going with that pistol in your hand like that?"

"Gotta see Jessie Mae," Cherokee Joe replied. "Gotta straighten things out."

"Straighten things out? What does *that* mean?"

"Might have to put her down, Jeff," said Cherokee Joe. "Might have to put her down," he repeated.

"Joe, this is crazy!" Ruby yelled.

"Ruby's right. This *is* crazy. You know the rules, Joe. We don't shoot women and children. Cool down a bit 'fore you go," said Big Jeff. Then he reminded Cherokee Joe about their next job. "And don't forget about the train!" he shouted in English. "You're the only one who knows what to do."

Cherokee Joe just continued arranging his stuff while mumbling to himself in Cherokee, a complex language neither Big Jeff nor Ruby understood. *I think it's allowed to shoot even a woman if she's an evil spirit,* he whispered several times. After getting his gear together, he tipped his hat to Ruby, and said to Big Jeff, "Adios, Cuz."

As Cherokee Joe strutted towards the front door, he noticed Abner standing in the storeroom doorway. Cherokee Joe shot him a side-eyed glare but said nothing. He unlatched the lock on the door and stormed out, clutching the whiskey bottle in his left hand.

Ruby burst into tears. "I shouldn't have said anything. I'm so stupid!" She ran to the window and watched as Cherokee Joe walked into the corral across the way. Big Jeff continued sitting in a stupor with his mouth agape for several minutes, as the sound of the trotting hooves of Cherokee Joe's Appaloosa, Spitfire, faded in the distance.

* * *

When Cherokee Joe arrived at Jessie Mae's place, the dogs out front greeted him with wagging tails rather than barking. When he walked in on Jessie Mae and the lawman, Cody Yates, they were frolicking in bed, the big brass one Joe had gifted her on his last visit. He held them both at gunpoint while on their knees, stark naked, on the bedroom floor.

"So, this is how you repay me after all I've given you?" Cherokee Joe asked. "Taking up with a lawman? Ruby was right, Jessie, you're a no-good harlot. I should blow your brains out."

"Take it easy, Joe. This ain't nothing serious. Just a *very* casual thing," Cody said softly.

Jessie Mae's eyes first widened at Cody's words. Then she squinted, looked at him, and exhaled. Crestfallen, with her head bowed, she stared at the floor. "You said you'd protect me," she said softly.

Cody looked Jessie Mae in the face. "I didn't know he would come while I was buck naked, Jessie Mae. What am I supposed to do, Jessie, shoot him with my . . . well, you know?" He looked down at his crotch, then up at Cherokee Joe.

"Really, Joe, this means nothing to me. I will gladly be on my way and forget I ever saw either of you."

Cherokee Joe grimaced and smacked Cody across the face with his pistol, knocking him flat on the floor. "Get up! Get up right now you yellow-bellied dog!" Cherokee Joe shouted.

Cody pushed himself up from the floor onto his knees. He gripped his face with one hand trying to slow the blood streaming from a gash on his cheek. Jessie Mae's eyes filled with tears.

"Where's the stash you promised to safeguard, Jessie?" Cherokee Joe asked.

"It's gone, Joe. All gone. Cody gambled it all away on the horses and blackjack. He said he would double it and . . ."

Cherokee Joe cut her off and stomped his right foot on the floor, "Horseshit!" he shouted. "All that money? Enough for my own ranch and a fresh start? That was a lot of damn money. There must be some left and I want to know where it is!"

"There's nothing left, Joe. Honestly. I didn't think you were ever coming back. There were rumors you'd been shot and jailed," Jessie Mae explained. "If I knew you'd be back for sure, I would have . . . I'll pay it all back to you, Joe. I promise."

"And I'll help . . ." said Cody.

"Shut up, Cody!" Cherokee Joe shouted. "Pay me back, huh?" He stooped over and looked into Jessie Mae's eyes. "How you gonna do that, lil' darling?" he whispered. "You gonna rob a few banks? A couple of stagecoaches, perhaps a train? I think not." Cherokee Joe straightened up and began pacing back and forth before his captives, breathing heavily. "I trusted you, Jessie. I thought we had a future together, but you're nothing but a lying snake. I don't believe either one of you thieving varmints. I think my money's here somewhere."

Not satisfied with their excuses, Cherokee Joe continued questioning Jessie Mae and Cody for another twenty minutes, demanding details of how, when, and where his fortune was squandered. When finally convinced it was, indeed, completely gone, an enraged Cherokee Joe cursed them both one last time and shot Jessie Mae clean through the forehead. "Bang!" Her body slammed backwards onto the floor. Cody jumped up and ran for the front door. "Bang! Bang!" Cherokee Joe shot him twice in the back before he got ten feet, and one more time for good measure in the back of the head as he lay sprawled on the floor. "Bang!"

Within minutes after the shootings, Cherokee Joe was mounted upon Spitfire, cantering at a steady gait towards his bandit hideout—the widow's place—six miles away.

* * *

Nelly Larson lived alone on two-acre lot covered in heavy brush and small trees. A narrow, bumpy, dirty path just wide enough to fit a buckboard wagon wound up from the main road to her property. An untrained eye could easily miss the turnoff from the road through the bushes since there was no sign posted at the entrance to the dirt path. But Cherokee Joe's eye was not untrained. He made sure no was around, then turned his horse through the bushes and up the steep path to the old widow's house. To his surprise, when he reached the clearing near the house, Miss Nelly, as they called her, was standing on the front porch holding her trusty shotgun.

"Well it's about time, Sonny," she said grinning.

"Ma'am," Cherokee Joe replied, tipping his hat and smiling. "I had to settle a business matter before heading over." He got down from Spitfire and gave Miss Nelly a hug.

"I heard some bad rumors about you. Knew they couldn't be true. But then again, one never knows," she said, patting him on the chest, still smiling. "The other boys are out back doing who knows what," she added, shaking her head back and forth. "They're antsy—as nutty as a squirrel with his tail on fire. You'd better go see to them right away."

"Will do."

"I'll ring for supper directly," said Miss Nelly, pointing toward the large bell hanging from the porch ceiling. "Chicken and dumplings. And no more gun play, Sonny. I had to remind them boys twice already. None. You hear me? You know the rules. They're going to bring attention to this place if they keep it up."

"Yes, ma'am, I hear you. Not one shot."

Cherokee Joe guided Spitfire by his bridle straps past the house, up the path to the ridge behind the house, and down the other side. At the edge of the clearing about thirty yards down slope stood a converted barn called the bunkhouse. His hideout. As he approached it, he heard Big Jeff tell the others that he had arrived. The guys should have been catching up on sleep but when he entered they were all sitting on their bunks, wide-eyed and frowning. Cherokee Joe greeted each one of them by name. He walked to the back window and looked out. The outhouse was still standing strong on one end of the field out back. On the other end, the horses were tied to a hitching post. Beyond the field, he could see the bank of the Concho River that marked the border of Miss Nelly's property. He then pulled a chair to the middle of the large one-room building and sat down. He pulled his Colt .45 revolver from its holster and began spinning the loaded cylinder round and round.

"I understand you boys been acting a bit antsy, huh?" Cherokee Joe said, still spinning the cylinder—staring at it, as if hypnotized. "Like you got a hot poker stuck up your rear? Is that right? Trigger happy? Disrespecting Miss Nelly's rules?"

"No, Joe. I wouldn't call 'em antsy. They're just a shy bit nervous, with you being gone. That's all," Big Jeff said. "Rufus and Crawford kind of lost their tempers over nothing—which bunk to use. You know, nothing. I managed to settle things down. Everybody's okay now."

"Well, Jeff, I hope that's all it was because I'm tired and mad. And right about now I'm ready to shoot anybody that messes with my business. We need this place and that old lady is like family to me. I used to run with her old man, Kit. After they hung Kit, she took me in for a spell and I've made sure she had enough to live off ever since. So calling attention to this place with gunplay over something stupid messes with my business and puts her in danger. I'm not going to stand for it. Y'all got that? If any of you boys got something you want to say to me, say it now." No one spoke up. "Okay, then" continued Cherokee Joe, "when Miss Nelly rings for supper, we're gonna go up to her place and have a nice meal—real civil and proper like. We're going pay her as agreed. Rufus and Crawford, y'all give her a little something extra for the trouble you caused and apologize. Then we'll come back here and I'm gonna layout the plan for the train job. After that I'm gonna get some sleep. When I get up tomorrow, I'm going down to that river and wash off some of this crust and dust. From the funk in here, you boys could stand a good washing, too. But anyway, afterwards we'll set things in motion to take the train," Cherokee Joe concluded. Then the dinner bell rang—one ring, "clang," loud and clear.

※ ※ ※

The *Angelo Express* from Fort Worth was roaring through the countryside about ten miles east of San Angelo when the track a mile ahead exploded at 10:17 in the morning. A huge cloud of smoke and dust leap from the ground into the sky like a volcanic eruption. The sound and force of the blast reverberated throughout the area rattling windowpanes and small structures, spooking farm animals and their owners, alike. The brakeman slammed the train to a stop well before reaching the damaged rails just as Cherokee Joe and his gang had expected. With rifles and pistols in hand, eight of the outlaws boarded the train, four from each side. One of them held the engineer and fireman at gunpoint in the locomotive, while four others stripped the rest of the crew and passengers of cash and jewels. The main prize, however, was in the locked and guarded car at the rear of the train. That's where the giant safe was located. At first the two armed guards inside refused to unlock the car's door. But when Cherokee Joe told them they would be burned alive or blown to smithereens if he had to dynamite the door, they opened it and surrendered their arms. Then Cherokee Joe and three of the other bandits pushed the safe through the side door of the railcar. The massive iron box, filled with thousands of dollars and other valuables, plunged into a nearby gully alongside a buckboard wagon. It took nearly the entire gang to drag and push it onto the buckboard that finally carried it away.

Twenty minutes after fleeing the scene of the stranded train, a smaller explosion took place a mile and a half away. This time it was the safe that exploded. Cherokee Joe and his men successfully blew the door open, but also damaged or destroyed a third of the contents. Nonetheless, there was still ample gold, silver, and cash to share—the equivalent of nearly two years of living expenses per man. They loaded their bounty onto their ponies and raced away, abandoning the empty safe and buckboard. After several miles of galloping, the horses were exhausted. But just as Cherokee Joe had planned, there were fresh horses for the gang at a pre-arranged location. They got onto those horses and continued their getaway at a slower pace, confident they had made a clean retreat from the crime scene.

* * *

The latest posse was organizing itself in *Miss Kitty's* saloon, speaking with Abner the bartender and among themselves, when the railroad track explosion occurred. Two days earlier Abner had telegraphed an urgent message to sheriff offices throughout the region about Cherokee Joe's gang and the imminent train robbery. Lawmen, gunslingers, and news reporters descended on San Angelo like a flock of buzzards about to feast on a dead horse. All Abner seemed to care about was getting his cut of the reward. He was trying to convince all of them to sign a paper agreeing to give him a share of the money before telling them any details about the location of Jessie Mae's place, what he knew about the train job, or the makeup of Cherokee Joe's gang.

"I heard them planning the whole thing, the dirty scoundrels," Abner had said to the posse. "I was ready to take them on by my lone self, but my shotgun was broke. I wasn't the least bit 'fraid of that bunch of scum," he boasted. "As soon as they left, I rushed to the telegraph office." Abner didn't actually know when or where the train robbery would take place, but he was doing a convincing job at making the posse believe he did. Then right in the middle of his little presentation, the explosion occurred. The giant cloud of smoke could be easily seen from outside the saloon. It was a clear sign something had occurred along the route of the Santa Fe railroad tracks. The posse of twenty-seven ran from the saloon, mounted their horses and headed toward the site of the explosion—leaving Abner in mid-sentence with a blank sheet of paper. Before the posse even reached the train, however, they heard the second, smaller explosion, but continued racing toward the train.

After examining the robbed and stranded trainload of passengers, the posse split up. Several lawmen stayed to assist with the train situation, the other twenty-two men headed in the direction the robbers had taken. They knew they were headed in the right direction when they came upon the buckboard, damaged safe, and, later, the first set of abandoned horses. It took them an extra day to catch up with Cherokee Joe because they didn't have fresh mounts. But on the second day, their Indian tracker, Bimisi, who had not exhausted his horse by galloping, returned to the posse after following the train robbers. He guided them straight to Miss Nellie's place, which he had previously snuck onto and inspected. He assured the posse that they were in a superior strategic position.

"In the main house there is an old woman, weak and probably senile. She did not see or hear me," said Bimisi. "The bandits are all in the bunkhouse beyond the main house. It's backed by the river. No escape route. No boats, only horses are back there. They will be easy to defeat. Like shooting fish in a barrel."

So the posse, led by a lawman called Marshal Stevens, headed from the main road and up the narrow bush covered path on horseback toward Miss Nellie's house in a single file. Before they got halfway, the bell on the front porch began ringing as if it were the end of time.

"Clang! Clang! Clang!" It was Miss Nellie's unmistakable alarm. As she rang the bell, she yelled. "They're here, Sonny, they're coming for you!"

Marshal Stevens, startled by the bell, screamed obscenities. He pulled his revolver and fired repeatedly toward Miss Nellie, striking her three times. The third bullet pierced her heart, killing her instantly. As she slumped to the porch floor, Cherokee Joe grabbed two revolvers. Then he and some of his men charged to the top of the ridge behind her house, while others rushed through the thick bushes running along both sides of the path from the main road. It was a maneuver Cherokee Joe had planned for them in case they needed it.

When Cherokee Joe realized the posse had killed the old lady, he raced toward them firing from pistols in each hand. First he shot Marshal Stevens. "Bang!" A bullet through the head—right between the eyes. The marshal fell from his horse onto the ground. Then Cherokee Joe fired on the man behind the marshal killing him instantly, as well. Within seconds, three other men on horseback rushed forward on their mounts, pointing their pistols and surrounding him. With blazing pistols in both hands, Cherokee Joe fired on the first man, killing him. He twirled and flipped to the right while firing on the second man, killing him too. The third man, at his rear, tried to aim directly at Cherokee Joe's bobbing head. Cherokee Joe, sensing the man, pointed the gun in his right hand over his left shoulder towards the man and pulled the trigger—but his pistol misfired. Click. Click. Nothing. "I got you now, you rattlesnake!" shouted the man with glee. With a tight two-handed grip he aimed carefully at the back of Cherokee Joe's head. Then, "Bang!" Cherokee Joe turned and watched as the man fell dead from his horse. Beyond the man's horse, stood Big Jeff, who had shot the man in the back. He winked at Cherokee Joe and hurried off to fight one of the other bounty hunters.

Further down the path, the posse's horses panicked as bullets from the bushes on both sides of them found their mark, dropping bounty hunters like sitting ducks. Those near the rear of the posse managed to turn their horses around. They galloped down the path, onto the main road, and fled in every direction. When the gunfire ended, twelve bounty hunters lay dead. Four taken out by Cherokee Joe. And except for Miss Nellie, none of the outlaws had been killed or injured.

* * *

After the gun battle, Cherokee Joe and his gang gave Nellie Larson a proper burial behind the house, but they left the bodies of the dead bounty hunters where they lay. They figured the posse would get reinforcements and return within a day or so anyway. If not, the buzzards and other scavengers would clean up the mess. The gang divided up the treasure from the train robbery and the loot Miss Nellie kept stashed in her house. Then they went their separate ways. Big Jeff and Cherokee Joe parted on somewhat of a sentimental note but promised to find one another in the future. "Maybe one day

I'll mosey on down to your chicken farm in Mexico," said Big Jeff, smiling, "and rescue you from your little wifey, and hound dogs, and snotty-nosed brats."

Within a couple hours of the shootout, Cherokee Joe was mounted upon Spitfire, heading south towards Del Rio and the Mexican border. After several days, he finally slipped across the Rio Grande into Mexico without incident. He greeted the militia guarding the Mexican side of the border in fluent Spanish, telling them he was a son of Mexico returning to his ancestral home and that he suspected he was being tracked by bounty hunters for unproven alleged crimes. They recognized his type and assured him they would resist any gringo posse that might be tracking him. In return, Cherokee Joe gave them a fist full of gold coins.

The commandant of the border guard, whose father was killed in the contrived American war that halved his country, told Cherokee Joe his battery of Gatling guns would "bite the asses of any gringo marauders so hard the bastards would not be able to sit down for a thousand years. With all my heart, I hope they come this way, Señor Cherokee." He placed his palms together in prayer fashion and looked to the sky, as if asking the heavens to send him the posse.

Cherokee Joe took leave of the border guard with gratitude and ambled along until he reached the village of Nacimiento de los Negros, where *Los Negros Mascogos*, the black Muskogee-speaking runaways under John Horse's leadership, had settled decades earlier. There Cherokee Joe found a host of relatives—cousins, aunts, uncles, and other descendants of John Horse and his associates.

Two months after settling in as a ranch hand, Cherokee Joe enlisted the help of a local bilingual schoolteacher in writing a heartfelt letter to Ruby Rose, begging her to join him. The letter was delivered to her by special messenger. Joe wasn't sure she would come, but she did. And they set up housekeeping in all the ways Big Jeff disdained, with children, hound dogs, and chickens in the yard. He learned from Ruby that the gang had indeed broken up for good. She said Rufus had formed his own gang, and Crawford had done likewise. As far as she knew, Big Jeff had headed west for California to do who knows what. "Every one of those rascals is being hunted by the law," she said.

Joe never rose to the legendary and heroic status of his grandfather, John Horse, but for many of the outlaws and lawmen of the Old West he still was a legend because he had redeemed himself, evaded the hangman's noose, and the bounty hunter's bullet. Not many outlaws as notorious as he ever achieved that end.

* * *

One year after the birth of their second child, Cherokee Joe took to the notion of solving the mystery of John Horse's disappearance. Against all advice to the contrary from Ruby and his relatives, he set out for Mexico City on horseback along the same trails his grandfather was purported to have followed.

After six weeks without having heard from Cherokee Joe, Ruby sent a search party of four men to find him. An innkeeper a few miles north of Monterrey confirmed *Señor Cherokee Joe* had been there. The man said on the morning after the first evening of his stay, Cherokee Joe insisted on going out to one of the nearby abandoned silver mines to investigate a local legend about a mysterious very old black man living in it.

"Some say he is an apparition. Others say he's real," explained the innkeeper. "I told Señor Cherokee that going out there alone was a very bad idea, but he didn't listen. He went and never returned," the innkeeper explained. "Twice I went looking for him without success. We still have his belongings. I don't know what to tell you. I am so very sorry for your loss."

The search team also visited several other abandoned mines in hopes of finding an injured or even deceased Cherokee Joe, but they found no sign of him. They returned his belongings to Ruby Rose and told her he had simply disappeared. "Poof! Just like a haint!"

※ ※ ※

Reader's Key:

Historical and Cultural References

Cherokee Joe — This character is partially inspired by the rock song, "Hey Joe?" recorded by various artists including Jimi Hendrix. It is about a fugitive from justice who has shot his unfaithful "old lady" (wife or girlfriend) and then says he's heading to Mexico to escape the hangman's noose.

John Horse — John Horse (mid-19th Century Black Seminole leader and freedom fighter).

Crawford — Crawford Goldsby, alias "Cherokee Bill" (mid-1890s multiracial outlaw).

Rufus — Leader of the Rufus Buck Gang, a mid-1890s multiethnic group of outlaws.

Miss Kitty's — Inspired by *Miss Hattie's Bordello* of San Angelo, Texas (circa 1902).

A Sorcerer's Mirage

SAMMY WAS SIPPING his third shot of whiskey when Wally Sahar arrived at the West End Tavern. At first startled by Wally's shoulder tap, Sammy hopped from his barstool to give his buddy a warm embrace. Sammy's own hair and clothes reeked of stale marijuana smoke, but to him Wally smelled freshly bathed and lathered in aftershave. And his crisp white dress shirt and classy style exuded success. Rather than taking a seat in the dark, musty bar, Wally asked Sammy to accompany him to the restaurant across the street. Sammy downed the remains of his whiskey in one gulp, wiped his mouth with the back of his hand, and followed Wally outside.

Sammy's bloodshot eyes squinted beneath the sun's glare as he and Wally made their way across the cobblestone avenue. Sammy's tattered jacket and scuffed shoes told the tale of a man on the losing end of society. And his worn heels, scruffy chin, and shaggy hair, cast him firmly among those who had given up all hope of improving their condition.

Wally led the way into the sparkling new Gaslight Grill. The ornate eatery sparkled like a Vegas showgirl. Polished silver, brass, and bronze foot rails, door handles, and window treatments glittered everywhere. It reminded Sammy of a jewelry store.

"This place is too rich for my blood, Wally," he said.

"No, it's not, Sammy. It's just an overdressed diner," Wally replied. "Nothing more than a burger joint with shiny doorknobs."

They chose seats in a corner booth, far from any snooping eyes and eavesdroppers. Unkept types like Sammy were not normally allowed in the Gaslight, but since he was being escorted by Wally, no one objected. Wally ordered the fish and chips lunch special for the two of them, and as they awaited their meal, he began discussing the business he had anxiously wanted to meet Sammy about.

"When I saw you yesterday near the train depot, I knew we needed to talk," Wally said.

"Sorry you had to see me that way, Wally," Sammy replied. "I didn't even know you were back in town. I don't usually panhandle, but this week has been a rough one. The rent is due, plus I needed money for a drink real bad. What can I say?"

"I understand, Sammy. You have to do what you have to do to survive. But it's not just the begging that concerns me. It's your entire situation." Sammy hunched his shoulders in response, as if to say, so what. "Are you working at all?" Wally asked.

"I've got this part-time gig," he replied. "It's an off-and-on kind of thing at a warehouse. You know—loading and unloading freight? It's better than nothing."

"Still living in that flophouse on Cambridge Place?"

Sammy nodded yes.

"I don't know how I ever lived like that," said Wally. "Twenty guys in a three-room flat with one outdoor toilet, sleeping on the floor like vagrants. That was tough. Must still be tough." Wally shook his head as if in disbelief.

Sammy rolled his eyes and said, "If I wanted somebody to bust my chops, I don't need you to do it, Wally. I could go to my parents' place for this. They're experts at sticking it to me. Especially Pops."

"You're right, Sammy. Who am I to judge, right?" Wally smiled and threw up both his hands as if to say he was from Sammy's world. "That's not why I wanted to see you and that's not why I asked about your situation. I asked to see you because I want to tell you about an opportunity—an opportunity to change your life for the better. It will put money in your pocket, food in your belly, and could even result in you having your own land, like a farm or ranch or something."

Sammy smiled and straightened up in his seat. "I'm listening," he said.

"When I left town last year, I told you I was going to visit friends, but I didn't say who they were or why I was visiting them."

"I remember. Very mysterious."

"The truth is, I had decided to join the Divine Expansion Movement," Wally revealed. "DEM for short. I wasn't sure I could make it through initial training, and I didn't want to come back disgraced if I failed. So, I didn't tell anyone I was joining. But I made it through. Now they've asked me to come back to tell others about it. You must have heard of DEM. They're conquering new territory like wildfire. Seems unstoppable. If DEM is as successful as I expect, it will provide freedom of opportunity and equality for everyone involved, regardless of race or social status."

"Yeah, I've heard of DEM," Sammy replied. "Four or five other guys have tried to talk me into joining. Almost got to me once. Some of it sounds kind of good. I've thought about it, but I don't see how it would help me, you know? A couple of my *DIM*-witted drinking buddies actually joined," Sammy said, laughing. "It's based on the notion of them having a divinely manifested destiny to spread their beliefs and authority over everybody, right?"

"That's right," Wally replied, "but only to establish peace and freedom."

"Wally, you know I haven't been religious since we were kids. I don't believe in that stuff anymore. I wouldn't last a week in DEM. I'm surprised you did."

"That's the other thing I wanted to tell you, Sammy. I've changed. I've been redeemed. I'm a believer man. If I can do it, so can you. I'm leaving soon to join the movement's latest military expedition and I thought if I explained it to you, you would go, too."

Sammy smirked and said, "So the rumors about you are true. *Wally's found religion*, they say. *Stopped drinking and smoking weed. Turned pious and upright. Ain't fun no more.*" Sammy chuckled. "I just dismissed it all, but it's true, huh? Now you want to leave on a military adventure and take me with you. I don't think I'm cut out for all that soldiering crap. Count me out, buddy boy."

"You don't understand, Sammy. The expansion movement truly is divine, and it's especially intended for people like us. It's what we've been waiting for. It's exactly what our parents and grandparents have been praying and searching for. We've never had *anything*, but now we can have *everything*. It's the opportunity of a lifetime to finally set things straight and have things our way."

"A divine mission, huh?" asked Sammy. "Where have I heard that before?"

Wally smiled and tapped his fingers on the table, as if nervous or slightly irritated. "I can appreciate your doubt," he said. "I was the same way, Sammy. But hear me out. Twelve months ago, my life was just like yours. You remember."

"My life's not so bad, man," said Sammy.

"Don't try to kid me. We're like brothers. I know you like the back of my hand. You're broke. You and others are living like dogs. You're twenty-two and still don't have a real job. When are you going to grow up and stop living like an orphaned teenager?"

"It's not like I haven't been looking for work. I just can't find anything, Wally. You know how hard it is for people like us to get hired. We're the last hired and first fired. The bigots call all of the shots," Sammy replied. "They've closed us out. There's nothing free and equal about this place. It's almost hopeless. Nothing to do but . . ."

"But drink. Drink yourself to death," said Wally, cutting him off. "I know how you feel, brother, but that's no solution. They've got you locked in a system that's purposely designed to keep you down and eventually destroy you. Drug and alcohol abuse, gambling in hopes of winning enough to live off of, these are all diseases of despair designed to kill you, Sammy. I felt the same as you until I met some of the guys from the movement and actually listened to them. They helped me see the light. They showed me there is in fact a divinely ordained path that could remedy my situation. And it can do the same for you, but you have to *listen*, Sammy. Just listen. It can put money in your pocket, instantly. Like magic! It can give *you* the power of self-determination, and free *you* from all of this mistreatment and oppression. You don't have to feel hopeless anymore. There *is* a way out."

Sammy's eyes widened. He sat up and leaned forward in his seat. "I wish there was a way out. Okay, I'll hear you out, Wally. I'll listen. Tell me more," he said, just as the waitress brought their meals. Wally looked side-eyed at her and waited until she left before continuing.

"I'll tell you all about it, Sammy, but first I want you to understand the spiritual side of what I think DEM is about. The mission is not just about chasing after material things. Materialism is not the objective. It's not just about putting money in your individual pocket. It's about creating a space for our people—but only for the believers among us who are willing to tough it out. And it's about fulfilling a vision of utopia, of heaven, right here on earth. I want to get you to embrace the ideals we're about. Otherwise, you won't be able to endure the struggle ahead of us. You know what they say, you've got to first cross the barren desert to reach the oasis of paradise."

"Okay, okay, I'm listening, Wally. Tell me about this spiritual angle. The ideals, as you call them," said Sammy, as he popped a piece of fried fish into his mouth.

"Don't take what I'm about to say the wrong way, Sammy, because I was in your shoes like—practically yesterday. But based on everything I know about you, you're headed straight to hell. The drinking, drugs, and all the other stuff, things you know our parents taught against, those things only lead to damnation."

Sammy waved his hand at Wally. "Yeah, yeah, I know, but where has all that righteous living gotten them? They work like slaves and get nowhere. Humph! It's hard out here. A guy's entitled to a little fun."

"I'll get to that in a minute. First answer this question, do you believe in hell, Sammy?"

Sammy hunched his shoulders. "I don't know," he mumbled. "Maybe."

"Well, you'd better be sure because it's one mistake you can't afford to make. But even if you don't believe in it as a place in the afterlife, you can't possibly deny that you're in a living hell right now, can you? You're unemployed, discriminated against at every turn, and for no just reason, whatsoever. You can't even rent an apartment. Abused by the police. Denied basic civil rights and social involvement. They do all of that to you, to us, and then make light of it as if our lives are a joke. Why would any self-respecting, sane people want to live under these conditions?" Sammy stopped eating and frowned, balled his napkin up and slammed it onto the table. Wally continued. "So, you're in hell now and if there's an afterlife, which I truly believe there is, then you're going to be in a worse hell when you die because you're violating every single restriction of our faith tradition. Both ways, man, you're in a messed up situation and I can't believe you want to continue living the way you are. You must hate yourself to want to continue living like you do."

"You really know how to blow a guy's high and ruin his appetite, Wally?" Sammy placed his elbows on the table and pushed his chin onto the interlocked fingers of both hands. He looked away from Wally, through the diner window, out into the street.

"Let me finish, Sammy. Don't be angry with me. I'm here as a friend, out of my concern for you. And there's a positive outcome to all this." Wally paused a second and gave Sammy a reassuring pat on the arm before continuing. "So, based on your current situation, Sammy, there's no escape from the hell you're trapped in. If you wanted to escape from your current hell you could kill yourself, but you're not sure what will happen after that, do you? I can tell you. Without a doubt, if you die for any reason before you're redeemed you're going into the eternal hellfire of the afterlife. The only way to avoid your ongoing hellish life and the much worse hell of the hereafter, is for you, my friend, to amend your ways and help in establishing a place where righteousness will prevail. To do that, we need a place of our own, our own state, where we would make the laws and run things. And what would we need to establish our own state? Come on, tell me, Sammy. What are the basic elements that we would need?"

Sammy shook his head. "I don't know, land and people, I guess," he mumbled.

"That's right, my brother, land and people. If we want the support of the people, at the very least we need a credible plan that promises to provide land and resources. They must have land to build houses and grow food."

"How would we get that much land? No one is going to give it to us, and we sure as hell don't have the money to buy it."

"That's so true, Sammy," replied Wally. "No, we have to do what every other land-hungry movement has done since the beginning of time. We have to take it from an inferior and unworthy people. There is no fertile, mineral rich unclaimed land in the world. Every place worth having is already populated by people, some of whom are undeserving heathens and devil worshipping infidels. So, it is our *divine mission*, our destiny and *right* to drive them from the land. The scriptures ordain this mission. God, Himself, commissions it. And it is *your* duty, Sammy, to support the cause. It is the only way to save your wretched soul, which is in hell now and will remain there unless you change, and is on the brink of eternal hell in the hereafter."

Sammy, still a bit groggy from the weed and whiskey he had consumed earlier, could not muster a logical counter argument to Wally's analysis. He pushed the thumbs of both hands into his temples, massaging them. "Wally, you're messing with my head, man." Sammy replied. "I see your point. I am stuck in a bad situation, but how do I free myself? Oh, God. What do I do?" he said, anguished and almost shouting. "What's next?"

"That's simple, Sammy. Next, you should join the DEM army that's conquering the territory needed for establishing a brand-new state. After you agree to enlist, we'll have to travel over a thousand miles to actually serve with the troops battling to drive the heathens from the land. Ultimately, we'll claim some of that land for our people and develop it into a place of peace and prosperity. Endless fertile fields, good homes, healthy families, money, self-determination, freedom! It's a magnificent vision, isn't it? Can you imagine it, Sammy?"

"When you lay it out like that, I guess I *can* see it. I never thought of the expansion movement like this, but if we could get some of land, we could have a good life."

"Not just a good life, Sammy. An excellent life! We can have huge farms like those north of here, and beautiful homes like those in the Uptown Estates. Endless orchards and abundant crops. No more racism and bigotry. As much work as you're willing to take on. As much money as you want. Can you feel the pride and freedom, and sense of redemption in that, Sammy? Can you see the vision that I'm seeing?"

Sammy nodded yes. "I can see it, Wally. I wish I had seen it like this before," he added, continuing to nod. "I want in!"

"That's good," Wally replied. "Very good. I don't think you'll have a problem getting in if you agree to sit through a couple of orientation sessions and pass a few tests." He took out a piece of paper, wrote down an address, and handed it to Sammy. "Meet me tomorrow at ten o'clock at this recruitment office," he said. He then pulled an envelope full of cash from his pocket. "Bam!" he said, slapping it onto the table. "Like I said, instant money—enough to cover your expenses until they ship you out. This is from me, as your dear friend. After you pass the tests and they send you to the DEM training camp, you'll start receiving regular monthly payments. All of your living expenses will be covered."

"Just me? Don't you mean us? Aren't we going together?" Sammy asked.

"I can't leave town just yet, but they need recruits like you as soon as possible."

"But you said, 'we this' and 'we that.' 'We together.'"

"We will be together as soon as I meet with a few other prospects over the next two or three weeks. The more recruits, the better. But don't worry, I won't be far behind. I'll catch up with you in no time, brother," Wally assured. "Then together *we*, you and me, will march to glory with the most exceptional army on God's green earth."

* * *

Following the meetings with Wally and his recruitment contacts, Sammy was approved to join the expansion movement. He was given a one-way train ticket to a faraway destination he knew nothing about, but he wasn't worried because he believed in DEM's vision of a better tomorrow.

After traveling over fourteen hundred miles by train to a designated pickup point, Sammy was transported to a training camp located on a vast desolate plain that looked like a no man's land. There he was given a uniform, boots, and other gear, and assigned a top bunk in the overcrowded barracks. Despite the overcrowded conditions, Sammy considered his situation better than it was in the three-room flat he had just left. After stowing away his gear and luggage, he and the other seventy-six new recruits were fed a supper of beef, beans, and bread in the mess hall. As they ate, their drill instructor laid down the law.

"Listen up, men! I am your drill instructor, Sergeant Hawkins. At all times you shall refer to me as 'Sir' or 'Drill Sergeant Hawkins.' From here on out, you belong to me," he warned. "For the next ten weeks, I own your sorry butts. When I say jump, you jump. If I say lay down, roll over and play dead, you roll over and play dead just like you're my dog. This is *not* a democracy. There is *no* voting, freedom of speech, or freedom of anything else unless I grant it to you. There shall be no outside communications, no unapproved letter writing, no music, alcohol, drugs, or unapproved reading material of any kind, including newspapers. Violation of these rules shall result in severe punishment. Unauthorized travel from the base will be deemed attempted desertion, subject to incarceration or execution. You go nowhere, and you do nothing unless I say so. Your day starts at oh-four-hundred hours. Lights out is at twenty-one thirty each day unless announced otherwise." When Sammy and some of the other recruits groaned, Sergeant Hawkins smirked. He then held up a sheet of paper and waved it around. "In addition to your combat and training exercises, you have been assigned weekly chores as listed on this task list, which will be posted on the information bulletin board inside of the barracks. Failure to complete your chores shall be considered insubordination and subject you to a range of penalties. That is all for now! Chow down, then return to your barracks. I suggest you turn in early because tomorrow will be a long day."

Combat training at the camp was harsh and nearly broke Sammy's spirit. The food was horrible, meager and insufficient. He was always hungry. While he managed to stay out of trouble, he witnessed other recruits being whipped, jailed, or verbally abused for minor infractions. One distraught recruit tried to sneak away from the base. He was tracked down ten miles away, brought back to the camp, and jailed indefinitely without a trial. It gradually dawned on Sammy that the men who had authority over him at the training camp were every bit as cruel as the bigots back home. Additionally, for the first three weeks in a row, Sammy was assigned to clean the latrines—the filthiest job on the base. One day while in formation, he made the mistake of asking the sergeant why he and the other three recruits of darker hue were always assigned latrine duty and the other dirty jobs.

"Are you questioning my authority, private?" asked Sergeant Hawkins.

"No sir, Drill Sergeant Hawkins!" replied Sammy. "You have the authority, sir. I just want to know why we're being discriminated against. I thought this army was supposed to be colorblind, sir."

"You *are* questioning my authority *and* being insubordinate!" yelled the sergeant. "For the duration of basic training you shall have permanent latrine duty. And one more word out of you about it will result in harsher penalties."

Despite the difficulty of combat training and the bigotry of the drill sergeant, to Sammy there were even worst aspects of the DEM training. Its mission was to invade, conquer, and claim for itself a land that was already inhabited. Therefore, it declared war on those inhabitants, vowing to remove or destroy them. Since no sane person would ever kill others, including children, for no particular reason, the new recruits had to be convinced that those people deserved to be slaughtered. So, similar to the strategy used by invading military forces since the beginning of time, the DEM army demonized their victims by indoctrinating its recruits to believe the indigenous people of that land were the enemies of good.

"Going back generations, we have known these idolaters as nothing less than devil worshipping enemies of all things good and wholesome. In fact, they are enemies of God, Himself!" declared one education training instructor. "On the outside these creatures look like men and women, but on the inside they are not fully human. Our only solution is to force them into permanent captivity and slavery, or to eradicate them from the face of the earth. You must understand that their noncombatants—women, children, and elderly—are as much the enemy as any of their warriors. If and when you encounter them, don't hesitate to open fire if they disobey. We must burn their dwellings, destroy their crops, and kill their animals. It's the only way to break their will. And whatever else you do, don't let them perform their rituals. Some of them engage in a supernatural devil dance that conjures up demons that can possess them and incite frenzied, almost unstoppable, violence against us. Don't ever allow it!"

Sammy felt trapped in an organization as mad as the society from which he fled. While he knew he wasn't the primary target of their madness, he also knew the madness could turn on him at a moment's notice by making one thoughtless comment or forgetting to fulfill a single chore. Every day he wanted to leave—either that or die. His life was far worse than anything he had been suffering back home. The cruelty, isolation, utter boredom, and stark surroundings comprised a new kind of hell that the recruiters never warned him of. The only thing that kept him going was the prospect of Wally showing up and somehow getting him released. But after seven weeks, Sammy realized Wally had lied and wasn't coming.

During the final phases of combat training, Sammy was required to learn how to use one of the latest machine guns. "This thing can mow down a whole village of those devils in no time flat," boasted his instructor." Sammy shuddered at the thought. The training was not something he expected or desired but his earlier superior performance in target shooting made him a logical selection whether he wanted it or not.

Upon completion of basic training, Sammy, now as lonely as ever, was deployed to the frontline as a machine gunner with a cavalry unit. It had just been ordered to join the hunt for a renegade indigenous tribe trying to avoid reporting to their assigned containment area. On the winter day he joined his unit, Sammy recalled Wally's sentiment that the people who inhabited that land were nothing but a bunch of savages, ungodly heathens blocking the righteous from establishing a society of freedom and prosperity. "Once we get rid of them our utopia can be established and our paradise will begin," he had said. *Yeah but first I'll have to go through another living hell*, Sammy now thought.

*   *   *

Under the threat of immediate annihilation by the DEM army, all of the indigenous tribal communities living within a seventy-eight square mile area had been ordered by emissaries of the divine expansion government to abandon their villages and property, including livestock, and to report by spring to specific reserved containment areas many miles away. Their fertile and mineral rich lands had been slated for redistribution to the settler population of the DEM government. Those being displaced were expected to travel to their designated containment area by foot over rough terrain and through harsh weather. Rather than reporting peaceably to their containment area, a "prison camp" they called it, three hundred and fifty-seven indigenous refugees—men, women, and children—under the guidance of their revered tribal leader, Chief Takoda, had instead chosen to run for freedom. They were headed for the closest international border about one hundred miles to the north, hoping that the other country, Canada, would provide them asylum and protection.

Sammy's all African American regiment was one of two regiments hunting down Chief Takoda's rebellious tribe. The members of Sammy's regiment were called "Buffalo Soldiers" by American Indians because the texture of their hair was similar to that of a buffalo rather than the straight horse-type hair of most other races. Because it was black, except for its white commanding officers, Sammy's unit was not allowed to march ahead of the white unit that it was partnered with. This was so, even though they were all fighting for the same cause— divinely ordained expansionism, under the doctrine of America's *Manifest Destiny* to conquer or control all of North America for God and Country.

After several days of relentless but tedious travel by horseback and wagon, the larger white regiment informed Sammy's unit that they had just received word that Chief Takoda's tribe had reversed course and was heading their way. Apparently, upon learning that American soldiers were closing in on them, the chief decided to surrender at their designated South Dakota reservation rather than face annihilation by the *Great White Father's* warriors. Colonel Francis Graham from the U.S. Seventh Cavalry personally visited Sammy's Buffalo Soldier unit and made it clear as to how the surrender and arrest of Takoda's people would transpire.

"We expect to encounter Chief Takoda and his people within the next day and a half where these two tributaries converge," explained Colonel Graham, pointing to an "x" on the map he had unrolled on a table inside of the tent of Sammy's white commanding officer, Colonel Jensen. "From there we're going to escort them about three miles to this open field where we'll set up camp for the night. They're likely to be half-starved but we're not going to feed them until they're disarmed. So, at the campsite the first thing we'll do is disarm each and every one of them of every firearm, knife, bow and arrow, and tool that could be used as a weapon. My men will assemble the prisoners in the middle of this field and execute the confiscation of arms by conducting a body search of every man, woman, and child, as well as a making a thorough search of all of their wagons and other property. Some of their young bucks won't like that and may resist. That's where your men will come in, Colonel. Your orders are to station your men in a semi-circle about forty yards from the assembly of these hostiles. Most of my men will be part of that semi-circle. Specifically, they'll be manning four Hotchkiss machine guns, here, here, here and here." Colonel Graham pointed to dots on the map. "I want your gunners to position themselves here and here," he added, pointing again to the map. "Between the gunners, position your best sharpshooters. I'll be observing the search from my mount nearby."

"With all due respect, Colonel, but do we need all that firepower for what seems to be a bunch of beaten down families that are voluntarily surrendering?" asked Colonel Jensen. "They're not coming to do battle. They're coming to turn themselves in."

Colonel Graham pushed himself straight up from the table and placed his right fist on his hip. He pointed and waved his left index finger toward Colonel Jensen and the other officers standing around the table. "You don't know these devils like I do. For generations my folks have passed down stories of how evil they are. They are the very children of Satan. They worship him and will engage in every deception to serve him and destroy us. Don't be fooled for a minute. They massacred Custer and defeated our unit, the Seventh Cavalry, using sorcery. It's the only explanation for their victory. And Chief Takoda is one of the leading fomenters of the resistance that is holding back the expansion. One of his tricks is to conjure up demons to attack us by dancing. So, I'm mustering as much firepower as we have to protect us from his black magic. I will not tolerate any disobedience from them, nor will I allow them to engage in their devilish rituals. If they rebel on any level, we must retaliate without hesitation. Don't you boys be fooled in the least by their fakery!"

"Colonel, you can't be serious. You don't actually believe in those tales of the supernatural, do you?" asked Colonel Jensen.

"There are great mysteries in the creation we don't understand, sir. And this is one of them. Now are you with me or must I relieve you of your duty?"

Colonel Jensen cleared his throat and softly said, "Sir, I'm with you. You're in command."

"That's right, Colonel! I am in command, so don't let me hear one more word from you or anyone else questioning my authority or strategies, do you understand?"

"Yes, sir!" replied Colonel Jensen.

"Good. You have your orders. We move out in an hour. That is all!" said Colonel Graham, who mounted his horse and galloped off toward his waiting regiment.

After Colonel Graham departed, Colonel Jensen had a short meeting with his own men and explained the strategy. Of course, he assigned Sammy to man one of the Hotchkiss machine guns in the semi-circle perimeter of the planned campsite. After the meeting, Colonel Jensen walked over to Sammy's Hotchkiss to inspect its readiness. While he was there, Sammy approached him.

"Sir, I don't feel comfortable about this assignment. I don't blame the Natives for wanting to be free. And now that they're turning themselves in, why treat them so harshly? It just doesn't feel right," Sammy explained, almost whispering.

"This is the army, private. You don't have to *feel* anything—right, wrong, or anything else. Just follow orders."

"But Colonel Jensen, suppose the Natives do or say something that's misunderstood, we're not actually going to shoot them, are we?"

The colonel looked around to see that no one else was nearby. "I understand your concern, private," he whispered, "but I don't think you have to worry. We're only making a show of force. No officer in his right mind would fire on unarmed people. So, for the last time, make sure your weapon is ready, take the position at the campsite you've been assigned, and follow my orders. If you don't, you may find yourself in a stockade or worse—at the end of a hangman's noose or before a firing squad. Do you understand? "

Sammy told the colonel he understood and with a knot in his throat, glumly prepared to move out with his regiment. He boarded his munitions wagon and guided it into the departing convoy. As the regiment began to roll out along the trail, the winter sun was high in the clear blue sky, but for Sammy the day was dark, as if an eclipse of malevolence had snuffed out any remaining shred of hope in his vision for a new life.

※ ※ ※

By early afternoon of the next day, the U.S. Army units arrived at the point where the two tributaries converged, as was reflected on Colonel Graham's map. Thick clouds blanketed the sky, the frigid air smelled of snow even though there was not a flake in sight. Two hours later, Chief Takoda and his followers began arriving at the location, as expected. The chief, an elderly man by any standard, was partially slumped over on his horse and wrapped in a blanket. He coughed incessantly. His eldest daughter, Winunna, who spoke fluent English, was at his side, attempting to comfort him. Colonel Graham informed the chief that his troops would escort the Indians to their reservation on the following day, but they had to travel several more miles that afternoon before setting up camp for the night. The chief accepted those terms, but nearly fell from his steed while speaking to his daughter about them. When Sammy saw that, he asked Colonel Jensen if it would be okay to transport the chief to the campsite in his wagon. After conferring, Jensen and Graham approved Sammy's request. Space was made by rearranging a number of items in his wagon and transferring others to another munitions wagon.

Chief Takoda and Winunna climbed into Sammy's wagon just as light snow began falling. The chief said something to his daughter in his native tongue, a language Sammy did not understand. Winunna turned to Sammy and wasted no time in thanking him.

"We are most grateful for your offer to transport my father," Winunna said. "I think he has pneumonia. He's coughing up blood."

"I'm glad I can help," Sammy replied. "I'm sorry to learn of his illness. He doesn't look well at all. No one that sick should be out in this weather, let alone on horseback."

Chief Takoda said something more to his daughter. "Hmm," said Winunna. "My father has asked why you and your black brothers serve in this army that is against us. He says the white man enslaved and oppressed you for many years, so why do you assist them in this evil?"

Sammy's jaw tightened. As did his gut. Winunna had asked a question he never wanted to confront. "I don't know, ma'am. I was told it's the right thing to do according to our holy scripture," said Sammy. "That we're supposed to take this land from the devil worshipping idolaters and make it available for those who follow the right and true religion," replied Sammy.

Winunna shook her head in disbelief. "So, your holy book says it's righteous to murder, rape, enslave, and steal other people's land? Is that what you're telling me? Because if that's what your religion says, I'm afraid *your* religion is the one that worships the devil. We don't worship evil in any form."

"You don't worship the devil?" Sammy asked.

"No, Sammy, we don't. But even if we did, wouldn't it be our right? How does someone else's peaceful practice of their religion give you the right to murder and enslave them, and steal their land? Does your holy scripture say that? Do your great prophets actually say such behavior is righteous?"

Sammy did not reply right away. During the pause, Chief Takoda asked his daughter what was being discussed. She replied to him at length. He asked her another question, which she transmitted to Sammy. "Father asks whether the enslavement of your very own people by the whites is justified by the religion you claim to follow? And I would like you to answer my earlier questions, as well."

As the wagon rumbled along, Sammy looked back briefly at Winunna, his eyes brimming with tears. One rippled down the right side of his face. "Tell your father that my understanding of my religion does not justify slavery. It's wrong now and always was. I see now the same holds true for what you asked, Winunna. Murder, rape, stealing land—all of it is wrong. Evil. The vision I was given of what is right was a false vision that twisted the truth."

"Well, I'm glad you're able to admit it. Maybe there's hope for you," she said. Then she turned and filled in her father, who responded. She said to Sammy, "Father says sorcerers have infiltrated every religion and philosophy. You can tell who they are because they always teach against what we are now discussing as righteous principles. They use seductive claims of being devoted to love, peace, and freedom, while committing acts of cruelty and violence. He says what you were given as a vision for a successful life was a sorcerer's mirage. One that vanishes in the light of truth." The chief then managed to yelp once in celebration. Sammy and Winunna smiled. "Are you going to stay in the army, Buffalo Soldier?" she asked.

"I don't think so," answered Sammy. "The army does many good things. It defends against foreign invaders and protects the builders of roads and railroads. I know it's not all bad, but I can't serve in this war against your people. It's against everything I believe in. I wasn't thinking clearly when I joined. So, I'm not sure about my future."

Winunna spoke again to her father at length. "Father says you must do what you feel is right in your heart and soul. He says certain things are clear—love, peace, honesty, patience, charity. They are universal principles. If you remain true to your heart, you will be free no matter what anyone does to you."

Sammy shook his head in agreement. Both Winunna and Chief Takoda then fell into a deep slumber, as Sammy continued driving the wagon. Awhile later, they arrived at the overnight campsite, as the snow fell heavier, and the temperature plunged.

***

At the campsite, Colonel Graham directed his men to assemble all three hundred plus Indians in the middle of the field, including Winunna and Chief Takoda, who was given a wooden box to sit upon. Those soldiers assigned to man the semi-circle of security were directed to take their positions. Dutifully, Sammy took position behind his machinegun. As soon as the men were in position, Colonel Graham commanded the Indians to surrender all of their weapons and tools to his men. The pistols and rifles were placed in one large pile, while bows and arrows, knives, tomahawks and any tool that could be used as a weapon were place in a second pile. But Colonel Graham still was not satisfied. He commanded all of the adult Indians to remove their outer garments in order to be body-searched for concealed weapons.

Chief Takoda, with his daughter's help, rose from his seat and spoke to the Colonel through Winunna. "This is unnecessary and cruel," he protested. "We have voluntarily surrendered to you. We mean no harm. You have all of our weapons. It is snowing and bitterly cold, and the people are hungry. Please show us mercy by allowing us to rest and eat."

"Tell the chief there will be no food or rest until our search is completed," said Colonel Graham to Winunna. "Strip off your blankets, coats, hats, and all other outer garments and prepare to be searched!" he yelled.

Winunna transmitted the colonel's message, but rather than shedding his blanket and coat, Chief Takoda began to chant. He grabbed his daughter's arm and began to shuffle his feet as if trying to dance. In short order other members of the tribe joined in. They held hands and formed a circle while chanting in their language to the Supreme Being for salvation from the soldiers, and for the peace and prosperity of yesteryear. A few of the women began to wail. While flailing their arms and spinning in circles, they howled lamentations of grief that struck at the very core of anyone who could hear them. Some shouted claims having visions of their ancestors standing in their midst. When the children joined in, it was more than Colonel Graham would tolerate.

"I order you to cease this demon conjuring right now!" he yelled several times. But the Indians ignored him. The humiliation of the strip search was obviously more than they were willing to endure, so they continued to chant prayers for salvation. "If you do not cease immediately, I will take all of you down, I kid you not!" Colonel Graham said. But the Indians did not stop, and the longer they danced and chanted the more threatening they seemed to anyone observing, except perhaps to Sammy, who watched in fascination. "Them natives done gone plum crazy," said a sharpshooter standing next to Sammy.

The snow began falling more heavily as the captive refugees danced and daylight quickly faded. Colonel Graham's men looked toward him, as if wondering whether he was still in control. From atop his horse he fumed, repeatedly pounding his thigh with his fist and gritting his teeth.

All at once one of the chanting, spinning women lost her balance and fell in a swoon upon the pile of confiscated firearms, setting one of the rifles off. "Bang!" The stray bullet did not strike anyone or anything. It flew up and across a nearby field and losing itself in the darkened emptiness. But its sudden crackle and fiery flash provided the perfect pretext for the colonel's next command.

"Fire!" screamed Colonel Graham. "We're under attack! Commence firing!"

To Sammy's horror, the sharpshooters and other machine gunners opened fire on the unarmed people standing before them. Sammy closed his eyes, placed his hands over his face, and crumbled to the ground on his knees, as his own unmanned weapon silently gathered snowflakes from the heavens.

Obliterated

A REAL-LIFE BOGEYMAN threatened to chop me into pieces. Dozens of witnesses heard him make the threat. It was made boldly and publicly, but none of the witnesses had the ability to defend me from him. They were too afraid. You see where I am from there were two kinds of bogeymen, a demonic mythical one for children, and a vicious real one for adults.

From an early age, the children of my country are told a folktale warning them against misbehaving. I was told the story many times, sometimes the long version with gruesome details, but mostly the shorter one that went something like this: *In the middle of the night bad boys and girls are stuffed into a burlap bag, whisked away, and later eaten for breakfast by Uncle Gunnysack, the Bogeyman himself!* In Haitian Creole he was called, *Tonton Macoute*.

While adults didn't believe in that supernatural bogeyman, they were quite familiar with the very real reign of terror inflicted on us by our dictator's national security forces that claimed to have voodoo superpowers. They proudly took for themselves the bogeyman nickname, *Tonton Macoute*, but unlike the goon in the folktale, these goons might come for anyone, at any time, day or night, and for any petty reason, especially a political reason. And if they took you away to their torture chamber, you might never be seen again. It was one of these vicious bogeymen that had threatened to chop me into pieces.

Early in his rule, Papa Jean, the dictator who ruled our country, assumed the title *President-for-Life* as if the people of Haiti had democratically elected him. What a joke! He ruled over the country with an iron fist. This is to say with the barrel of the gun and a machete. He ordered the Tonton Macoute to punish or imprison anyone who expressed dissent against him in any way, even jokingly. Therefore, all opposing political parties or political views were outlawed. In short, he did not believe in freedom of speech or any of the other freedoms enjoyed by much of the world, including modern America. Every few years, however, he orchestrated a national presidential election. He "won" each one by an astounding ninety-nine percent of the vote. An examination of the pre-checked ballots in his favor attested to his victory. To this day, no one knows who cast the one percent of opposing ballots. They were probably bogus. But none of that meant very much when I was starting out because I was a non-political person. All I wanted to do was to be left alone to run my business in peace. But the bogeymen had other ideas.

* * *

In my section of Port-au-Prince, they called me "Mr. Fix-It." As a youngster I was fascinated with mechanical devices and household goods, like bicycles, watches, and even furniture. If it had to be assembled, I wanted to know about it. If it was broken, I did my best to fix it. I guess you could say it all began when I was nine. That's when out of sheer curiosity I dismantled my grandfather's precious silver pocket watch with small screwdrivers. I wanted to see what made it tick. So, naturally I had to open it up. When I did, I could actually see the gyrating mechanism inside. The "movement" they call it. It blew my mind. But that wasn't enough for me. I wanted to see how all of those tiny parts interacted. So, I pulled some of them out, one by one, until the watch stopped working. I was so proud I grinned from ear to ear. Then it occurred to me that grandfather might not share my joy when he saw I'd killed his watch, so I feverishly went to work trying to bring it back to life. Let me tell you, it's a lot harder to get the guts of a watch back inside than it is to take them out—especially when you don't know what you're doing! It must have been an hour or more, after many tries, before I finally reassembled that watch and snapped the back of the case cover into place. I reset the time and pushed in the stem. To this very day, the sweetest ticking I have ever heard came from my granddaddy's "fixed" watch. I was so proud, but it would be years before I told anyone in the family about that victory.

From watches I graduated to other devices. By the time I was twelve I was fixing neighbors' bicycles for a small fee or nothing at all. I fixed clocks, chairs, the wheels and axels of carts, toys, and even musical instruments. I was a natural. So naturally, I was known as *Mr. Fix-It*. At sixteen, I opened my own shop on the side of our small family home using random boards and an old wooden door. It was nothing more than a tacky little shed, but it was mine. I was content fixing the broken hopes of other people, bringing them renewed joy, while earning enough to help my family survive. That is until the bogeymen started coming around.

Like the gangsters of America's Roaring Twenties, all across Haiti the Tonton Macoute extorted money from small neighborhood shopkeepers like me for many years. "Protection payments," they called it, meaning protection from being beat up or burned out by them. Government officials, including the police, were no help against them because they feared the Macoutes as much as everyone else.

Since Haiti was such a poor country, a small monetary payoff each week was enough to keep those thugs satisfied. But eventually I grew tired of being abused so I went around to the other shopkeepers in an attempt to organize a resistance to the extortion by establishing a shopkeepers union. I even considered organizing some kind of general strike that would last until the thugs left us alone. "Instead of giving our money to the Macoutes, we can use it to pay for legal representation and other organizing costs. This way we would determine how our resources are used. It is the democratic way," I said to each neighborhood business owner in one-on-one private discussions or sometimes in small groups of three or four. Of the twenty-two nearby shops, all of the owners agreed with me about wanting to end the extortion, but only a few of them expressed an interest in supporting an organized resistance and establishing a union.

"Who's going to protect us from their revenge?" asked Mr. Roland, the shoemaker.

"We must protect one another," I answered. "If we form a union we can organize and support our own militia! They would not dare attack any one of us if they know all of us would rise up against them. And we can fight against so many other things too. Unfair taxes, the price of goods and raw materials, illegal fines, and even chronic shoplifters. We can form a truly powerful association, like they've done in France and North Africa."

"Well, I've never heard of a shopkeepers union, but the idea does sound nice. Real sweet, young man, but I don't think it will work here," Mrs. Trudeau the baker said to me during a visit. She shook her head and frowned. "The Macoutes are all over. There are hundreds of them. They will come down to our neighborhood and burn us out! We'd be lucky to escape with our lives. For my part, I'm going to continue paying them. I suggest you do the same and not start any trouble. Consider yourself lucky you even have a shop."

The shoemaker, the barber, the baker and fruit vendors, all expressed doubt and fear about my organizing plan. In fact, I suspect at least one of them informed the Macoutes that I was stirring up trouble because one stifling afternoon a bogeyman came to my shop. He was a stranger to me, not the regular gangster who collected the payments.

"I want to buy this bicycle," said the Macoute as he rubbed the handlebars of the bike leaning against the outside wall of my shed. His mirrored shades hid the coldness in his eyes. His mouth, fixed with a permanent frown, barely moved as he expressed his wish.

"Unfortunately, that bicycle is not mine to sell, sir" I replied. "I just fixed the gears. It belongs to one of my customers—a delivery man who uses it to transport the goods of his own customers."

The Macoute pulled his shades partially down the bridge of his nose so I could see his eyes. The cold dark void of his inner self became clear. *Boo! Do you see how ruthless I can be?* his soul said to me. "This is not a request, boy," he said. "I need a bike, so I will be buying this one."

"With all due respect sir, that bike is not mine to sell," I said anxiously. "So please unhand it and leave me in peace."

"Leave you in peace?" he shouted. He pulled his machete from its sheath and waved it around. "I'll leave you alright. I'll leave you in pieces . . . if you don't sell me this bike! In fact," he said pulling a sum of cash from his top shirt pocket, "here's a dollar." He threw the money on the ground. "Consider this bike sold!"

He then put his machete away and mounted the bike. As he began riding away, I grabbed my big rubber mallet, the one I use to tap sensitive mechanical parts into place, and I chased after him. Within a few yards I caught up with him and slugged him across the back of the head with the mallet. I must have hit him very hard because he fell from the bike instantly. I managed to keep the bike from slamming to the ground, but the bogeyman banged his head against the ground like a rock falling from the heavens. There he remained unconscious for several minutes, spread eagle on his back. While he was out cold, I removed his pistol and his machete. I threw his machete into my shed. I clutched his pistol in my right hand and watched him from afar. I knew he wasn't dead because he was breathing heavily and groaning. By the time he regained consciousness, a crowd from the neighborhood had gathered around him. Those in the back of the crowd hurled insults at him, calling him a thieving dog, a coward, a swine, and a bully. Others had spit in his face while he lay knocked out. By the time he lifted himself from the unpaved dirt road, I had returned the bicycle to my shed and was standing next to it with his pistol in one hand and my own machete in the other.

The bogeyman wiped the spittle from his face with his shirt tail and hands. He winced as he rubbed his right knee, which had apparently been bruised and bloodied when he fell. He looked around for his missing shades and straw hat and hobbled a few feet over to them and put them back on. Then he reached for his pistol only to discover an empty holster. An empty machete sheath on the opposite side of his waist told him he was weaponless. I stared him down and waved his pistol in the air, daring him without words to come toward me. He pointed at me and shouted out a voodoo curse for my doom. Some of those in the crowd gasped. Many people believe the Macoutes have supernatural voodoo powers, but I never believed it. So, I shouted the same curse back at him and by the motion of my outstretched arms I again dared him to come toward me. Instead, he began walking backwards from where he was standing and made me a solemn promise.

"Dimanche!" he shouted. "You dare attack a Tonton Macoute and rob him of his rightfully purchased property? Before the setting of the sun you will find yourself in the bowels of Fort Dimanche, Mr. Union Organizer. Mr. Fix-It Boy. We know who you are. I will slowly chop you into a thousand pieces. This I swear. Dimanche!" he said again, referring to Haiti's death camp prison of savage abuse, where blood runs from one cell to the other like a river. He then turned and hobbled away as fast as he could on his injured leg, as the watching crowd jeered and laughed at him.

After the Macoute left, a number of people urged me to immediately flee Haiti. These included members of my family, a parish priest who heard about the incident, and two of my closest friends. Mama not only urged me to leave, she insisted on it. "The Macoutes will return for you today," she said, "so you have to go into hiding now and leave the country on the first available boat. If you don't, they will not only arrest you, they might take all of us to Fort Dimanche. We must be able to tell them with conviction that you've fled. Even so, we will have to return the pistol and pay them a ransom to leave us alone. In the meantime, son, you must go! Seek political asylum in the U.S. or one of the other island nations," she said as tears streamed down her face. I felt as if I had made an awful mistake that endangered my loved ones.

Like everyone else, I knew that many thousands of people had been tortured, murdered, or died while confined in Papa Jean's torture chamber. There, as many as forty people were routinely packed into a single cell and forced to use one open pit toilet. Everyone slept in filth on banana leaf mats that served as coffins when someone died of starvation or torture. The prison guards would just roll the body up in the mat and dump it into an unmarked mass grave somewhere. Ultimately, there were many reasons to flee Haiti, but I only needed one—to keep my family from being imprisoned in Dimanche. So, with the help of my friends, I quickly arranged for the return of my customers' property whether fixed or not. Then I gathered some of my personal belongings, and as much cash as I was able to borrow and beg from my family. Within hours of my fight with the Macoute, I had hopped a crowded bus heading to the northwest region of the country where most of the refugee boats depart for America. That was in the first week of July, 1980.

It was not difficult to find a boat heading for Miami. A mass exodus of tens of thousands of people was underway. They were fleeing Haiti for political reasons or economic distress caused by corrupt politics, and the owners of boats of every size and type wanted to cash in on the opportunity to make quick money. Jean Pierre, the captain of *My Baby*, a forty-foot wooden fishing vessel that I bought passage on, took nearly all of my cash but he still could not tell me how long it would take his sailboat to reach Florida. "It depends on many things," he said, "the weather, pirates, law enforcement, and even a possible accident. If our luck is good and the sails hold out, with strong winds it may take a week or so, but I can't be sure." Nonetheless I agreed to his terms, and along with forty-two other anxious passengers, we set sail at the break of dawn on the day after I reached the Northwest.

* * *

The first day on the ocean was rather uneventful but still very uncomfortable because we were crammed together and unable to move freely. There wasn't enough room on the deck to allow all of the passengers to lean back along the vessel's sides, so many of the men took turns sitting out in the center of the deck, where we leaned against one another, back-to-back. It was almost unbearable to sit like that for long periods. And what I thought was good weather—calm, clear, and sunny—turned out to be a problem because the wind wasn't strong enough to push us along as quickly as we had hoped. Plus, the searing midday sun eventually made us feel as if we were being cooked alive. Those wearing hats were at an advantage. I soaked one of my towels in fresh water and draped it over my head. Others did the same. It helped tremendously.

On the positive side, we had plenty of food and water, which I'd heard was not the case on many other refugee boats. But the fact that we were seemingly floating in one spot was beginning to mess with my head. Captain Jean Pierre said were moving about three miles an hour—knots he called them. One man complained he could swim faster than that. I think he and the captain were the only ones who could swim at all. Well, I can swim a little but not very well. I'm okay in a swimming pool but the notion of swimming in the open sea frightened me to death. At the swimming pool I can see who and what is in it. I can even see the bottom. But when we were out on the ocean, I couldn't see much below the surface. All I could think about were the things down there that could kill me, like sharks and strange creatures that no one knows about. I had never been one who wanted to sail upon the ocean at all, especially in a rather small vessel. But there I was because there were also things on the land that could kill me, like that bicycle bogeyman and his henchmen. So now my only hope was that the boat wouldn't sink and the wind would push us more quickly to our destination.

The first night on the water was terrifying. I sat or stood with my eyes wide open the entire time, and every time there was a large splash I bit the side of my hand to keep from screaming in fear. I couldn't tell what was splashing out there. A whale? A shark? Some grotesque creature from the darkest recesses? I couldn't tell. The full moon reflected off the water allowing us to see quite a distance across the surface, but it wasn't the same as daylight. It was during that first night that I reconsidered religion. I'm sure I prayed to the Lord and several saints to help us make it through the night.

On the second day, four of the other passengers were starting to get on my nerves. The old woman I was permanently forced to sit near kept singing spirituals about the sweet bye-and-bye or the fire and brimstone that all us sinners were going to suffer in the afterlife. It was bad enough that she sang of death and torture, but she had the most horrible monotone, nasal singing voice that grated on everyone nearby. We begged her to stop but that only encouraged her to sing more. I'm quite sure she was a sadist because the more we suffered the happier she seemed to become. She sang and sang until she was out of breath. I actually prayed in gratitude to the Lord for designing the human body to run out of breath.

When I asked that woman why she was even on the boat, she told me she was a former nun, turned Pentecostal, who was fleeing poverty and religious discrimination. I told her she should have stayed in Haiti because she could have made a ton of money working in one of the Tonton Macoute's torture chambers. Then I said to the other passengers while pointing my thumb towards her, "I'm sure any prisoner would tell the Macoutes whatever they wanted to know if it would stop this *Singing Nun* from actually singing." Everyone laughed at my joke except her. I think she may have even whispered a Voodoo-Catholic-Pentecostal combo curse on me. Then she continued singing undeterred by my criticism, and even more loudly whenever I was seated next to her.

And then there was the non-stop talker. He apologized to us all for his constant chatter about the most mundane things that came to mind, from his sinus congestion, to his constipation, to the escapades of his cheating ex-wife. He explained that whenever he was nervous he had to talk ... and talk ... and talk. If I had been married to a person like him, I'm sure I would have cheated and deserted him, too. *Le Professeur*, the only passenger who had been to college, called the talky-talk guy, *Mr. Loquacious*—or *Monsieur Loquace*, in French. No one knew what loquacious meant, but it sounded offensive enough, so we called him that while pleading with him to just, "Shut up!"

The other two particularly annoying passengers were two babies, an infant girl and a boy toddler, that cried constantly. All of us understood that the babies could not help themselves. Hell, I felt like crying myself, but nonetheless they were massively annoying to me because they reminded me of my own pain.

For a quick minute, I was even tempted to hop a ride on one of the two rickety boats that passed us on the way back to Haiti from Florida and the Bahamas after having successfully smuggled their passengers. The torture of the annoying four was that bad, but not bad enough to make me do something so crazy as to surrender myself to the bogeymen of Fort Dimanche. But I do recall this: I had decided that if for any reason we had to throw a couple of people overboard in order to save the boat and the rest of the passengers, the Singing Nun and Mr. Loquacious were at the top of my shortlist. I figured they could console one another by singing and talking incessantly while holding hands on the way to the ocean floor. I felt not the least bit of guilt about wanting to rid us of those two. After three days of the same, however, I began getting accustomed to the annoying four as well as to the surreal plain of endless waves that had become my new home. By then I no longer had the urge to strangle the annoying adults. And even the babies had become less annoying because they cried less frequently. Captain Jean Pierre said we had traveled quite a bit by that time, more than two hundred and fifty miles. I found this comforting. With continued friendly winds pushing our sails, we were expecting to reach Miami in less than five additional days.

* * *

It came out of nowhere on the fourth day at sea. At mid-morning the sky was cloudless, almost magical, but by noon the ominous clouds of the monstrous storm were on the southeastern horizon rolling our way like a runaway locomotive. I asked Jean Pierre if he had life jackets for us. He answered no. I asked if he had any life ring buoys in case someone fell overboard. Again, he said no. I complained about his lack of emergency planning. He said I was wrong and proceeded to give everyone long pieces of rope and instructed us on how to tether ourselves securely to the boat's railings and mast and how to avoid the swinging boom. He told the parents of young children to tether themselves together. Silently I cursed myself for not having asked him about such a vital matter from the outset. I would never have gotten on his boat with such inadequate emergency equipment. So, there I was on the high seas with a killer storm practically in my face and only then did I think about emergency planning.

"*My Baby* has survived some of the fiercest storms in the history of the Caribbean," Jean Pierre said, trying his best to reassure us. "I have seen many much bigger than this one," he said pointing toward the storm. "If you can stay aboard, you'll survive. If you fall overboard . . . well," he warned, trailing off, while making the typical sign of the cross upon his forehead, shoulders and chest. Several of us men helped him take down the sails before tethering ourselves. Then we sat or crouched along the deck silently in the listless waters, staring at the approaching storm, awaiting our fate.

When the storm arrived, she didn't disappoint. Choppy waters transformed into huge, merciless waves within minutes. Thick clouds blocked all sunlight as day became night. *My Baby* rocked and rolled and was tossed from one giant wave to another, as thousands of gallons of seawater washed across the deck. The angry sea strove mightily to snatch each and every one of us into her depths. Sadly, it was successful ten times. Poorly tied tethers came loose in the soaking rain and seawater. Seven men, two women, and the baby girl were gobbled by the sea. By the time the storm passed an hour later, the rest of us, half drowned, were emotional basket cases. Stunned, we gazed at one another and into the clearing sky above. The only person who seemed to have maintained his sanity was Jean Pierre. "Unbind yourselves and help me bail water overboard!" he commanded. "We're going to be alright now." Only a few of the men complied with his guidance and request for help. I, like most of the others, opted to remain tied to the boat for about another half hour.

After bailing as much water as possible, Jean Pierre made a head count of everyone and checked off the names of the missing from his passenger list. He said he would try to inform their families when he returned to Haiti. He also gave us other bad news. Two crates holding half of the remaining fresh water and food were washed overboard during the storm. And as if that weren't enough, he saved the best for last. He wasn't sure where we were because we had been twisted around dozens of times during the storm. "We've blown off course. After my cracked compass dries out, I'll have a better idea," he said, "but we can't be too far from the coordinated path because the storm was a relatively short one."

Jean Pierre conducted a solemn memorial service for those lost at sea. Perhaps the saddest part was the heartrending tears and anguish of the man who lost his wife and baby. He and two other men had tried to hold on to them, to no avail. For the remainder of our sojourn there would be no jokes, funny stories, or laughter. Both the Singing Nun and Mr. Loquacious remained silent for a full day before sounding off again. The ten deaths and loss of rations assured our continued sense of acute insecurity.

Eventually, Jean Pierre did get *My Baby* back on course and a strong wind kicked in, pushing us forward at record speeds. By the time we reached the coastal waters off Florida four days later, we were half starved and desperately thirsty but feeling confident of our prospects for survival. His plan was to await dusk before going any further, and to sneak into a hidden dock near Miami under the cover of darkness. No sooner had Jean Pierre told us the plan that the unmistakable and increasingly louder sound of helicopter rotor blades announced the rapid approach of American law enforcement. The helicopter seemed to shoot through the air like a bullet straight toward *My Baby*. As it got closer it swooped down like a raptor and hovered above. All of us looked up. *United State Coast Guard* was emblazoned on the side of the red and white aircraft. "You are in the territorial waters of the United States of America," the booming voice from the whirlybird's speakers announced. "You are under arrest. Do not attempt to move from this location."

An expression of resignation washed across Jean Pierre's face. "We are caught!" he shouted as loud as he could, trying to speak above the noise of the aircraft. Frowning, he turned in the direction of Florida and pointed at the speedboat slicing through the water toward us. "The police on that boat will take us into custody," he shouted. "Tell them you want political asylum. That you are afraid to return to Haiti for fear of torture and arrest. Maybe they will let you stay."

The helicopter continued hovering above as uniformed officers from the U.S. Coast Guard's heavily armed gunboat pulled alongside us and announced they were coming aboard. After speaking to Jean Pierre briefly, they said they were taking us into custody. They attached heavy ropes from their boat to *My Baby* and towed us to a Miami dock not far from the newly opened Krome immigration detention center, where we were later processed and interviewed.

※ ※ ※

The detention center was crowded and noisy, but I had my own bed to lie upon. We were given real food—a welcome change from Jean Pierre's dried fruit, beef jerky, hardtack, and off-tasting water. And the bathroom and shower facilities were heavenly compared to my funky unwashed situation on *My Baby*. Amid the noise and commotion of the center, I slept like a baby for nearly ten hours straight on the first day. That being said, it was still a prison no matter what fancy name they assigned the place. I was given a blue prison jumpsuit to wear and assigned a number. I was not free to do as I pleased, and I could not leave. I was jailed for suspicion of conspiring to enter the U.S. illegally. After six days in detention, I had my first official interview or, more accurately, interrogation, by a man who introduced himself as Officer Morales.

Aside from verifying basic data such as my name, date of birth, etc., Officer Morales only wanted one thing out of me, that being my agreement to voluntarily return to Haiti since, he claimed, my only basis for coming to America was to escape economic deprivation.

"Haiti it the poorest country in the Western Hemisphere, one of the poorest in the world," Officer Morales said. "Naturally you and your people want to leave there and come to the U.S., the richest country on earth. But that's not how our immigration system works. You can't just sneak into this country because your country is poorer than ours. Lots of countries are poorer than America. So, I ask again, would you rather languish in detention for a year or more and then be sent back to Haiti, or immediately return voluntarily?" he said. A translator named Mr. Mercier transmitted to me in Haitian Creole everything Morales had been saying in English. If I had agreed to leave, I would have been given a free plane ride home. But of course, I could not agree. As both Mama and Jean Pierre advised me, I said I wanted to apply for political asylum.

"On what do you base your claim for asylum?" asked Officer Morales. I explained how I was nearly robbed by the Tonton Macoute. "That was merely a personal business dispute with one of your potential customers. I cannot accept your claim based on that," said Morales.

"But it was much more than that," I argued. "This Macoute threatened me with torture and death at the Fort Dimanche Prison."

"Of course, he threatened to arrest you. He was angry about your having assaulted and cheated him. People who attack police officials should be imprisoned," said Morales. "The torture allegation, well, I'm not sure I even believe he said that to you."

"But Officer Morales," I said through Mr. Mercier, "I was trying to lawfully organize a shopkeepers union to protect us from extortion and abuse. I can obtain sworn statements to support me on this issue. The Macoute who tried to rob me specifically mentioned my union organizing activity. How could he know about that unless he was targeting me for political reasons?" Mr. Mercier translated my statement and question for Officer Morales and shook his head, yes, in knowing agreement with me, which he really wasn't supposed to do. He raised his eyebrows and looked Morales directly in the eyes as he spoke. "If I am arrested and interrogated by the authorities upon my return," I added, "I am quite sure I will be sent straight to Dimanche because my name is surely on their special list of political enemies and I did not have permission to exit the country."

Thousands upon thousands of Haitian refugees were being sent back to Haiti because they didn't know how to assert a claim for political asylum. Many were arrested upon their return to Haiti because they had left without permission, like I had done. In Haiti, no one was supposed to leave the country without an exit visa. To do so was considered a crime. Authoritarian governments across the world that consider their population to be government property, impose similar exit restrictions on their citizens.

Officer Morales, satisfied with the conviction of my claim, smiled and said after I completed a full application for asylum he would recommend my temporary admission into the United States pending a final decision on my claim. I was allowed to confer with a representative from a nearby Haitian relief center who assisted me in completing my asylum application. Three days after the interview with Officer Morales, I was released from the detention center into the streets of Miami with a photo identification card and a work authorization permit. I was told the decision on my application ultimately would be based on a full review of my sworn affidavit, those of witnesses which I had to obtain from Haiti, and an opinion from the U.S. State Department regarding conditions in Haiti and whether it believed I had a well-founded fear of persecution if I returned there.

It took the State Department over a year to issue its letter of opinion regarding my asylum application. The letter said I did not have a well-founded fear of persecution because the government of Haiti, one that is friendly to the U.S. and supports the fight against the spread of communism, was no longer persecuting union organizers as a distinct class of dissidents. The letter said the Haitian government had apprehended and subsequently stamped out all members of that formerly persecuted class. "The class to which the applicant claims to belong no longer exists. It has been completely obliterated. Therefore, he cannot and will not be targeted as a *member* of a nonexistent class," stated the opinion letter. The State Department recommended my application be rejected and that I be deported back to Haiti. In denying my application for asylum, the immigration service accepted and endorsed the State Department's recommendation. By letter I was advised I could voluntarily depart to Haiti or report to immigration court for a deportation hearing within sixty days of the date on the denial letter, in which case the U.S. government would incur the cost of transporting me to Haiti.

I was both astounded and devastated by this decision and the unsuccessful appeals that followed. None of the other asylum applicants at the relief center could believe the illogic upon which the rejection of my claim was based, but the director of the center said she had seen this type of perversion of reason by the U.S. government many times. I decided that I certainly would not return to Haiti, neither voluntarily nor under the watchful eye of immigration law enforcement. It was clear to me that federal agencies could not be trusted to issue a just decision in my case. My only choice was to go underground. I decided to take my chances living illegally in America than dying "legally" in Port-au-Prince.

Now after decades of living in the shadows of the American dream, I am a New York-based father, grandfather, and great-grandfather to African American boys and girls, and men and women, all of whom are of Haitian heritage. But I suppose I shall forever be considered "an illegal" by the U.S. government because I have not yet been *obliterated* by the government of my home country.

Story Notes

Introduction

These notes provide cultural insight and references for various aspects of the stories in this book. They may prove useful in conducting research and assisting readers in understanding the forces that compel people to become refugees and migrants. As in the stories themselves, I have tried to use these notes to bridge the reality of past and current black life in America to the plight of people on the move in other parts of the world. And since black American history is, indeed, an inseparable and fundamental ingredient of the American experience, these stories and notes may be used to demonstrate that the nation as a whole is connected to the treatment and condition of young refugees and migrants universally.

Before reading the notes for a story, you are advised to first read the story, itself, because in several cases the notes reveal twists that if known in advance may diminish the impact of the story as it unfolds. I also share through these notes my motivation for writing each story to demonstrate how culture, politics, and even tragic events can influence an individual's literary expression by compelling him or her to confront humanitarian concerns.

Dash!

This story is a fictionalized account of an actual event and features a historical figure, John Horse, who was a remarkable personality. In this respect, *Dash!* is a nouvelle à clef, which is a short story (with an optional "key") that features real people who may have fictional names. In this case I thought it was important to use John Horse's real name because I suspected that few readers would be familiar with him and his mission. I invented for him a favorite child, Arabella, whose anxiety as a young black girl running for her life from American soldiers determined to enslave her would have affected him profoundly, as it would for any father under those circumstances.

The number of refugees led into Mexico in 1850 by John Horse and his partner, Wild Cat, vary in the historical accounts from under two hundred up to three or four hundred. Regardless of the actual number, it's likely there were among them many young black and Indian girls—all of whom would have been sold into slavery and sexually assaulted if caught by the dragoons sent to capture them. In considering that possible outcome, I concluded that if I were a young girl like Arabella I would have chosen death over capture. So, I built this into the storyline.

Initially I was motivated to write *Dash!* by, among other things, the plight of the Yazidi refugees of Iraq who fled on foot toward Kurdistan in 2014 from the terror, rape, and enslavement of the so-called Islamic State (I.S. or ISIS) army that pursued them. The Kurds, with dilatory American military support, eventually defended many of the Yazidis but not before hundreds of them had been executed or captured as sex slaves by I.S. But the Yazidi girls and women were not the only ones to have suffered such a horrible fate in recent times. Similar modern tragedies helped drive the development and completion of *Dash!*

During the mid-1990s, there were the Bosnian Muslim girls and women of Central Europe, many of whom were literally raped to death in sex camps operated by the Serbian Army. And shortly before the Yazidi crisis, there was the 2014 tragedy of the missing schoolgirls of Chibok, Nigeria—nearly three hundred of whom were kidnapped and enslaved by Boko Haram, another so-called Islamic army. In 2017, the Muslim Rohingya women and girls fleeing rape and murder by the Burmese military garnered international attention and collective condemnation.

While the world is quite aware of these modern atrocities, it is either ignorant of or has discounted the reality of similar horrors that were inflicted in one form or another upon African Americans by their own government and fellow Americans. The story of Arabella brings history to life and compels every nation to measure its touted virtues against its own history and to justify its responses to modern international humanitarian imperatives.

Questions for Readers to Consider: Arabella is extremely bright and intellectually advanced, but she still plays with a baby doll. Does it seem credible that a highly intelligent twelve-year-old girl or boy to play would play with dolls, action figures or other make-believe items? If not, at what age should she or he be forced to stop and why? What about other make-believe activities such as paintball or Civil War reenactments, for example—should they be prohibited beyond a certain age? Was it right for the old woman to encourage Arabella to kill herself? Why did the government of Mexico encourage thousands of refugee slaves to migrate there; was it out of a humanitarian concern or were there other motives? Are there still Afro-Mexicanos in Mexico and the Southwest?

If so, how do they look, where do they live, and what is their legal status under modern Mexican law?

Brother Man

During the mid-1800s, many Quakers living in the Southern United States were held in contempt and regarded with suspicion by their slave-holding neighbors because they were outspoken abolitionists. They dressed and spoke differently, and they had their own peculiar house of worship—the Meeting House. Some of them paid with their lives and property for supporting the Underground Railroad or for attempting to smuggle slaves belonging to their neighbors to the North.

I was motivated to write *Brother Man* after reading online accounts of Joshua Hoge, a Quaker who lived in Loudoun County, Virginia during the 1850s. His slaveowner neighbors despised him because of his beliefs about freedom for all people and had very little to do with him. And they suspected his involvement whenever a slave went missing, and especially so because Hoge did "an awful lot of traveling to Ohio," in his wagon. *Brother Man* celebrates the Hoge-type person and his/her love of freedom for all. See Eugene Scheel's, *Journey to Freedom was Risky for Slaves and Guides*, featuring Hoge and others. (Washington Post, May 27, 2001; https://www.washingtonpost.com/archive/local/2001/05/27/journey-to-freedom-was-risky-for-slaves-and-guides/a68f68bf-58f1-4ca6-84a2-58bf7bf7779d/; last accessed Dec. 24, 2019).

Through this story, I also attempt to validate the presence of religious minorities in America who, though often different in style and language, have embraced the principles of

American freedom and democracy while enduring seemingly endless ethnic and religious profiling and discrimination, even as they stand up for justice for everyone. The Quakers endured similar discrimination not so long ago. This attests to a quote attributed to Mark Twain, "History doesn't repeat itself, but it often rhymes."

While I did not find evidence of the adoption of a law banning Hoge from traveling outside of the county without permission, attempts by the federal government in 2017 and beyond to ban the travel into America of people from specific countries that are majority Muslim demonstrated how religious bigotry could be practiced through restrictive travel laws. I would not be surprised to learn that the use of similar legal mechanisms occurred to the neighbors of Quakers suspected of supporting the abolition of slavery.

For their part, many male slaveowners routinely assaulted their enslaved women, girls, and even their men and boys, sexually. There was no legal remedy for such assaults because generally under the law a slaveholder could do as he pleased with his "property." While such a person could be socially ostracized for abusing a child slave under nineteenth century age of consent laws, a person, whether slave or free, was determined to be old enough to engage in sex if he or she met the minimum age of consent. In many states it was ten years old. In some it was even younger or a little older. And many states and territories had no minimum age of consent whatsoever. This means if a child was "of age" and protested she had been forced by a much older man in a court of law, it would be her word against his. Rarely would all white male juries or judiciaries accept the testimony of a black person, let alone a black child, over that of a white defendant. So, at age ten, little Sadie of the story had become vulnerable for abuse by Will Bishop without him having to fear any legal or social consequences.

American age of consent laws of the nineteenth century seem absurd and shockingly low to most of us today, but from the days of antiquity until the early twentieth century they were the norm in most societies across the earth. Primarily it was organized American women who fought male legislators endlessly to raise the age of consent in every state during the late 1800s. Some legislators rationalized their resistance against protecting little girls from sexual availability by grown men on the basis of there being a "degraded race" in America—enslaved black people, whose constant and early procreation enriched their economy. Imagine the horror of being a young girl or woman owned by someone who thinks like that; who has absolute power over you; who is motivated purely by self-interest, lust, and profit. We see this type of man, and sometimes woman, among us today in positions of power. Imagine if he actually "owned" people and what he would do to them with impunity.

I suspect many modern-day critics of ancient marriage customs would be disabused of their sense of inherent Western superiority when they realize that some of their own great-grandfathers and other forefathers likely engaged in relations with little girls as young as ten and even younger, especially if they were slaveowners. For more on the evolution of age of consent laws in America, see, generally, *Purity Crusade: Sexual Morality and Social Control, 1868-1900*, David J. Pivar (Greenwood Press, 1973).

Questions for Readers to Consider: Clearly, Brother Man was stealing the property of his neighbors—namely their slaves. Is it ever morally right to lie, cheat, and steal, especially if you purport to be a righteous person? In a democracy, where laws are supposedly adopted and enforced under the power of duly elected officials, is it ever right to resist or even violate the law based on one's personal values? Were the leaders of Lovettsville right in trying to monitor and prevent Brother Man from stealing their "property"? Why did Will Bishop "hate" Brother Man for being different even though Brother Man had never done anything to him? Is it ever okay to dislike someone for being culturally different? Who was the historical figure, Benjamin Lay, and what happened to him when he condemned his fellow Quakers, as well as others, who participated in slavery during America's colonial period?

Shamika on the Bridge

The main character of this story, Shamika, represents the type of urban resident who is constantly struggling for the basics of life—adequate food, clothing, and shelter. Of course, there are millions of residents in non-urban regions all across the country facing the same dilemma on a daily basis. But this story just happens to be about a city dweller. In it she is struggling to remain in her lifelong and historic rowhouse, even as her friends and family are forced to migrate to the suburbs. Because they can no longer afford the skyrocketing rent, ever-increasing real estate taxes, and the gourmet supermarket prices of their rapidly gentrifying neighborhood, they have no choice but to move away.

I first encountered my very own Shamika—the individual who inspired this story—and several of the other characters in the story, including Stamp Man and the Begging Widow, at the turn of the century in a tacky, rundown Giant Supermarket in one of Washington, DC's gentrifying neighborhoods. That store has since been demolished and replaced with an upscale one. I've yet to encounter a Shamika-type in the new store but I have encountered more than a few people like her in well maintained suburban shopping centers near neighborhoods where forced-out migrants from the DC inner-city have relocated. So in this regard, the fact that Shamika of our story is trying to transact business in the new upscale supermarket is not farfetched. In fact, the problem of SNAP benefit recipients attempting to negotiate transactions like those that Shamika engages in has become so widespread in suburban stores that many DC-area markets now have signs posted on the front door warning against it.

 Nonetheless, the challenges faced by Shamika and people like her are real. She has endured hard-knocks all her life, yet she fights on by balancing herself on the bridge between two worlds and working the political and financial systems that imprison her, to her advantage. Everyone who lives around her is a migrant or potential migrant, either moving in or about to move out. She knows she will have to leave one day but, in the meanwhile, she fights tooth and nail for her dignity and the survival of her family. When the person I modeled her on approached me in the old supermarket, her appeal was powerful, confident, direct, clear, and virtually irresistible. She was respectful but unyielding. And highly intelligent, yet delivering her appeal using the language code of her target, whether street idiom or nuanced modern standard English. She was a professional. I suspect few have the constitution and level of know-how to do what she does, and that supermarket was her turf for that particular hustle.

While that person, my real life "Shamika," did not tell me that her partner/husband was imprisoned for marijuana possession, over time I have encountered so many other true stories about disproportionate marijuana-related prison sentences being metered out to black men that I easily envisioned the repercussions of such injustices playing out in Shamika's life. So I incorporated it as part of her motivation to hustle. Likewise, Becca's privileged background, which shielded her from imprisonment for the very same crime as Jamal's, has been expressed repeatedly in real life. See the work and statements of Adam J. Foss, a criminal justice reform activist, for a comprehensive treatment of this phenomenon. For example, at approximately minute fourteen of the "Degree of Impact" episode of the PBS series "Roadtrip Nation," Foss briefly describes how race and economic privilege can influence whether a person is prosecuted. That episode may be accessible online.

Questions for Readers to Consider: Can people like Shamika and Becca truly live in harmony as neighbors? Who is responsible for urban gentrification and the forced migration of the less fortunate that it causes? In one city, long-time residents filed a so-called "Gentrification Lawsuit" against the city government for $1 billion. They allege that city officials have discriminated against poor and working-class residents of color by supporting new housing development in their neighborhoods and adopting new policies to attract young, affluent professionals to live in the expensive new housing. The outcome of the lawsuit is pending, but do you think long-time residents should have the right to prevent expensive new housing and business development (gentrification) in their neighborhoods? If not, what can be done to protect everyone's rights?

Nathan's Ark

The Great Migration was among the largest internal migrations in human history. It took place in the United States in two phases between approximately 1916 and 1970, when over six million African Americans moved from the South to the North and West, fleeing racism and poverty, very much like many twenty-first-century refugees and migrants across the earth have done. In Nathan's Ark, I envisioned a refugee/migrant teenager who flees the backwoods of the South for New York, where he soon discovers and embraces his bliss—his mission in life as a writer.

Secondarily, through this story I attempt to incorporate several significant aspects of the African American experience and American history, generally. For example, in the fall of 1919, the largest mass lynching in American history occurred in Elaine, Arkansas. Often called the Elaine Massacre or Elaine Race Riots, it resulted in hundreds of African American men, women, and children being summarily executed by white mobs roaming the vicinity of Elaine. Immediately preceding the attacks, black sharecroppers were in the process of unionizing because of perceived abuses by white landowners.

While the fictional lynching of Nathan's parents necessarily takes place several decades after the actual Elaine Massacre, this story is meant to memorialize that tragic event. It depicts a common situation that motivated many African Americans to flee in the middle of the night. Like Nathan, many of them ran for their lives after having been warned not to leave without the permission of the white landowners for whom they worked. Sadly, most of the refugees and migrants from the South encountered conditions in the North that were nearly as brutal and unjust as those they left behind. Discriminatory housing practices forced many of them into decrepit tenement buildings and public housing projects plagued by building and health code violations, and sociological pathologies—street gangs, drug addiction, alcoholism, unemployment, and de facto segregated school systems. And some were preyed upon by the meanest of their urbanized neighbors, who held them in contempt. Acting and being "country" was not cool, slick, or refined according to many of the urbanized. Thus, new arrivals were often swindled or gratuitously assaulted.

Lastly, this story is a pastiche in homage to the late poet and short fiction writer, Henry Dumas, an Arkansas native, whom Toni Morrison called a literary genius. He is the author of *Ark of Bones* and *Riot or Rebellion*, and many other short stories. Aspects of those two stories, in particular, are the inspiration for elements of this story. Nathan is from Arkansas. In the dream segment, he envisions a train of dead souls in the middle of a cotton field that somewhat parallels Dumas' mystical ark of souls in his surreal *Ark of Bones*. And in Dumas' *Riot or Revolt*, the LeMoor Brothers Bookstore and one of its proprietors, Micheval LeMoor, which are likely modeled on the late Lewis Michaux and his Harlem-based *African National Memorial Bookstore*, are central features. Likewise, a proprietor called "The "Professor" (Michaux's real-life community nickname) and his bookstore are featured in this story. The story ends with Nathan and the Professor leaving the 1967 Black Power Conference in Newark, less than a week after that city's rebellion, insurrection, or riots. If he didn't witness them, both historic events were likely at the forefront of Dumas' developing political and literary consciousness. At the very end of the story, Nathan promises the Professor to seek out Sun Ra, who, of course, was a mentor and friend to Henry Dumas.

Questions for Readers to Consider: What is meant by finding or identifying one's bliss? Have you identified your bliss? If not, how are you going to do so and when will you begin pursuing it? Can you change your bliss over time or have more than one? Who exactly was Henry Dumas and how is his killing the same or different from current police shootings?

The Legend of Cherokee Joe

Most of the black cowboys and settlers of the Old West were law abiding citizens hoping for a fresh start. Some were lawmen, trackers, and even bounty hunters. But, as Arabella put it in *Dash!*, "some of them were bad." Unfortunately, in this story one such bad person turns out to be her very own orphaned son, Cherokee Joe.

In this *nouvelle à clef* (short story with a key), historical figures and places are included to illustrate the causes that motivated marginalized youth of the past to form gangs that engaged in criminal enterprises. They had no respect or trust in the social and legal systems that gratuitously abused them, so they chose to become outlaws. As it was then, so it is today. Of course, choosing a life of crime is always a poor choice that usually ends badly.

During the days of the Old West, also called the "Wild West," whenever law enforcement began closing in, many fugitives from justice sought refuge in Mexico, just like the protagonist in this story; or they ventured further into the lawless west like Big Jeff.

Questions for Readers to Consider: Is there ever sufficient justification to form or join a gang? What is the difference between a gang and other organized groups? Don't they do the same things for members? Is there a way to address the needs of today's youth so that they would not seek support through gangs engaged in criminal enterprises? What were the guiding principles that motivated Cherokee Joe to want to leave his gang? Do you think he realized his goal of achieving a better life? Why did he go in search of his missing grandfather, John Horse? What is the current political and social condition of Afro-Mexicanos in Mexico?

A Sorcerer's Mirage

One of the consequences of America's war on Iraq was the rise in 2011 of the so-called Islamic State army (also known as I.S., ISIS, ISIL, and Daish). Its leaders claimed to be divinely ordained to conquer an expansive portion of the Middle East in and around Syria called the Levant, and to govern it under a draconian interpretation of Islamic law. They also mischaracterized many of the inhabitants of the region as devil worshippers who were under the spell of a sorcerer. Similar claims were lodged against American Indians by American settlers.

Few observers expected I.S. to last very long, let alone achieve the measure of success it ultimately realized. Surprisingly, tens of thousands of disenchanted Iraqis and other Middle Easterners joined that movement. And even more surprisingly, hundreds of Americans and Europeans traveled thousands of miles to also join. This both fascinated and baffled me. Why would someone leave their hometown in the United States or the United Kingdom and travel thousands of miles to join I.S., with all that it implies? As it turns out, many of them, like Sammy in the story, felt marginalized and abused by racism and income inequality in their own societies. They believed the enchanting online I.S. recruitment videos promising prosperity and equality—even heaven on earth or utopia.

Upon arriving at the I.S. military boot camps, however, many returnees and escapees reported they encountered less than ideal conditions that often included racism, sexism, bad food, menial job assignments, extreme boredom; and on the frontlines they witnesses beheadings, rape, torture, the enslavement of women and girls, and they faced execution if they tried to leave.

During America's expansion into the West (the "Westward Expansion") in the 1800s, a similar driving concept was invoked to instigate war and recruit an army. It was called *Manifest Destiny* and under it the government justified the ethnic cleaning of tribal lands, resulting in the Indian Wars, unspeakable atrocities on all sides, and the establishment of Indian reservations and countless broken treaties. One of the most infamous military acts during the expansion period was the largest mass shooting in American history, the 1890 Wounded Knee massacre of over 150 men, women, and children by the U.S. Army.

America's Westward Expansion army included segregated regiments of African Americans called Buffalo Soldiers, some of which were engaged at Wounded Knee. Why would an African American leave his hometown in Baltimore or New York, for example, and travel hundreds or even thousands of miles to join the United States Army in its war against Indian tribes in the West? This is what Winunna and Chief Takoda did not understand of Sammy in the story? And, further, what did the typical real-life Buffalo Soldier encounter upon reaching the frontline of the Indian Wars? Historical accounts chronicle shameless racial discrimination against those men and even violent attacks on them for attempting to patronize white-only saloons and other recreational and comfort facilities. So why join such a mission?

In developing this story, I discovered that Buffalo Soldiers often were motivated by the same incentives that attracted American and European I.S. recruits—promises of equality, prosperity, and salvation. To claim their reward, however, both types of soldier were ordered to commit atrocities bordering on genocide and other acts that would be defined as war crimes under modern international law. Of course, such soldiers eventually become disillusioned upon realizing the vision they had been shown was merely a mirage. If they were fortunate, they were able to leave the movement and return home with minimal damage or injury. If not, they plunged into a pit of perdition like Sammy. [*Special Note*: The name of the man who persuaded Sammy to join DEM, Wally Sahar, in Arabic loosely signifies the title "Sorcerer Friend." While Sammy, or "Sami" in Arabic, signifies in this case "one who has been elevated" or who is "lofty" in consciousness.]

Questions for Readers to Consider: What happens to a soldier who refuses to follow orders on the battlefield? As a soldier, would you be able to refuse an order to commit a terrible act? What can a society do to keep its members from chasing a mirage by joining a movement devoted to killing others and stealing their land? Many American Indian tribes were enemies to one another and sometimes committed atrocities, as well. Some also committed atrocities on white settlers. Does knowing this change your view of the Western Expansion and its ensuing Indian Wars?

Obliterated

This story illustrates yet another aspect of the American reality for black refugees and migrants. As a young attorney during the mid-1980s, I worked for a free community legal clinic that represented scores of political asylum seekers from several African countries, Haiti, and El Salvador. During that period, tens of thousands of Ethiopians were fleeing famine, unemployment, and civil disorder that consumed the country. Simultaneously, many thousands of Haitians were fleeing Haiti primarily by boat to escape abject poverty, as well as violent political oppression by the government. Their harrowing plight was very similar to that of the refugee boat people from Syria and North Africa that began streaming into Europe in 2015, under what is called the European Migrant Crisis or European Refugee Crisis.

One of my law clinic clients was a young man from Ethiopia. He claimed to be an active member of an outlawed political party advocating changes to his country's one-party communist government. Similar to the unnamed protagonist in *Obliterated*, my client had been threatened with arrest. He managed to avoid apprehension even as the country's security police were rounding up all party members. He escaped Ethiopia by somehow obtaining a U.S. student visa and made his way to Virginia even though he did not have a required Ethiopian "exit visa" stamped in his passport.

Obliterated fuses the refugee motivation for asylum, i.e. fear of persecution, with that of escaping dire economic conditions. In the case of my Ethiopian client, we submitted voluminous evidence to support his fear of persecution if he returned to his country. His application was strong and seemed to be destined for approval. The immigration office needed only one additional document before making its decision—an advisory opinion on the application from the U.S. State Department.

Upon receipt of the advisory opinion months later, I accompanied my client to a meeting with an immigration officer for a final review of the application, including the State Department's advisory. At that meeting, the immigration officer told us he was shocked to have received a letter from the U.S. State Department advising him to deny the application for asylum on grounds that the government of Ethiopia had systematically arrested all known members of the political party that my client had belonged to and that they and their party had been "obliterated." Since that outlawed party no longer existed, the State Department reasoned, the young man could safely return home because no one would be looking for him.

By law, the immigration officer was allowed to disregard the advisory letter for good cause. When I pointed out the implications of sending someone back to a country to be obliterated, as suggested by the advisory opinion, the officer became infuriated. "This opinion is ridiculous!" he said, almost shouting. "I'm disregarding the State Department's recommendation and granting asylum immediately," he added, shaking his head.

My client flashed a broad smile, but I managed to contain my surprise and joy behind an expressionless gaze. At the close of the meeting, I politely thanked the officer for his understanding and assistance. Unfortunately, like most applicants, our Haitian protagonist in the story was not so fortunate with his immigration officer.

Questions for Readers to Consider: Should international borders be open to anyone, including refugees and migrants, without restriction? Should international borders be eliminated altogether? What if, for example, the borders of a country are opened to anyone and a nearby country takes advantage of it by expelling all of its own homeless people, prisoners, and severely mentally ill patients to that open border country? Something very similar occurred in 1980 during the Mariel Boatlift, when President Jimmy Carter agreed to accept massive numbers of refugees fleeing Cuba. The U.S. government later discovered the Cuban government had emptied its prisons and psychiatric hospitals and mixed in thousands of violent criminals and mental patients, along with the other refugees, on the boats.

Within the United States, some state governments reportedly are exporting their homeless and poor to other states such as Florida, Texas, or Hawaii. By encouraging such residents to accept a small amount of cash, a set of new clothing, and a one-way bus, train, or plane ticket to another state, the state of origin can eliminate the cost of continuing to support them. Should shifting the burden of support like this be allowed domestically? Should it be allowed internationally? If so, under what circumstances?

Acknowledgments

This collection was one of ten finalists for the 2018 Katherine Anne Porter Prize (short fiction) and was long listed for the 2017 Santa Fe Writers Project Award.

Thanks to all the marvelous people at my publisher, *Unsolicited Press*, especially Esme Howler, who believed my stories are worthy of sharing with the world, and the team of editors who reviewed and improved the manuscript.

Thanks to my beloved wife and partner, Ismat, whose unfaltering support and patience made it possible for me to devote the time and resources required to complete this project.

Thanks to my dearest granddaughter, Jasmine, whose young adult sensibilities and candid opinion allowed me to refine this collection in ways I would have never imagined.

Thanks to John McNamee, whose unrelenting encouragement inspired me to continue writing narratives that, in unexpected ways, contrast humanitarian crises of the past against ongoing humanitarian concerns.

Thanks to the many family members, friends, and associates who provided invaluable feedback and editorial suggestions over the years for one or more of the stories in this collection, including Ismat Abdal-Haqq, Qadir Abdal-Haqq, Margot Aronson-Levin, Veronica Britto, Phyl Green, Safiyyah Jabali-Nash, Regina Lowe, John McNamee, and Tyrone Mitchell.

Special thanks to the Transcendent One, the ever-present force that instills in each of us a consciousness of purpose, then grants us the gifts required to pursue our mission.

About the Author

Irshad Abdal-Haqq writes fiction and nonfiction. Through fiction, he endeavors to transform common cultural misperceptions by revealing the links between our past, present, and evolving intercultural relationships—especially those involving marginalized communities. Irshad's nonfiction has included award-winning essays, community newspaper articles, and several scholarly articles. He publishes an online literary journal, and for over seven years published a groundbreaking scholarly journal—the Journal of Islamic Law and Culture.

In addition to his other activities, Irshad has a singular focus on creating a vital missing literary component to the American canon. Through memoir, fiction, and creative nonfiction, he aspires to chronicle the African American Muslim perspective on transitioning from a Black Nationalist social reform movement into mainstream American culture. It was a historic transformation that has yet to be expressed adequately through firsthand creative literature.

Irshad was born in Newark and raised in the Greater New York City area, but now calls Washington, DC home. He is a graduate of Amherst College (B.A.), Georgetown University Law Center (J.D.), and Antioch School of Law (M.A.T. Clinical Legal Education).

About the Press

Unsolicited Press is a small publishing house in Portland, Oregon and is dedicated to producing works of fiction, poetry, and nonfiction from a range of voices, but especially the underserved. Our team has published books that aren't afraid to take on topics of race, gender, identity, feminism, patriarchy, mental health, and more. The team is comprised of hardworking volunteers that are passionate about literature.

Learn more at www.unsolicitedpress.com.

CPSIA information can be obtained
at www.ICGtesting.com
Printed in the USA
LVHW050709020523
745785LV00004B/540